No one on board Space Lab I realized what was happening. The Com Officer was transmitting the captain's detailed report on the solar flare to Earth; the captain himself was finishing a plastic bottle of coffee while he wrote up his log. No one knew, then, that the Hellmaker had been activated.

HOT ROD rolled on its center of gravity and its beam-director mirror swung in a huge arc. Internally, the communications beam to Thule Base had been interrupted, fail-safe units did not respond.

The mighty beam lashed out. The vibrations of the directing mirror began placing gigantic spots and sweeps of irresistible energy across the ice cap of Greenland.

By the time the servos refocused the communications beam on Thule, there was no Thule . . . only a burnt-out crater.

Someone or something had unleashed the Hellmaker.

CHALLENGE THE HELLMAKER

by

WALT & LEIGH RICHMOND

ace books

A Division of Charter Communications Inc.
1120 Avenue of the Americas
New York, N.Y. 10036

CHALLENGE THE HELLMAKER

To Rusty
". . . It was never a fair
fight, you know. They had the guns,
but we had the habit of independence. . . ."

PROLOGUE

Mike stood in the crowded blockhouse waiting to be called to the shuttle. Through the narrow ports he could see only the top of the rocket, overshadowed still by its gantry; could spot the flash of sunlight as the entryport opened to admit passengers delivered by a spidery elevator in ones or twos.

The crowd in the blockhouse thinned slowly, until he was alone except for the U.N. Security guards that composed a large part of any activity at the project base. He moved restlessly, waiting.

At last his name came over the intercom. He stepped through the heavy door, felt it swing to behind him, and started toward a jeep that waited, driverless but its motor idling, to carry him to the rocket.

"Blackhawk!"

The harsh voice brought him to a stop in midstride, and he turned to face a security guard, gun drawn. As he turned, a figure brushed to pass him, knocking him slightly off balance as it headed towards the jeep.

"You are under arrest. . . ."

Mike's hand grasped the arm of the passing figure, his foot went behind its knee, and as the guard's gun spoke it was the stranger's body that was before it, and Mike was to the side.

Without a break in his movements, Mike slammed into the guard, the edge of his open palm coming down onto the other's neck in a karate chop. The guard's body slumped in slow motion across the stomach of the other.

For a second Mike stood looking down at the two crumpled figures, wondering whether the gun had been *set at lethal charge, or only to stun.* Then his eyes narrowed at the familiarity of the face before him, and abruptly he realized that it was to all intents and purposes his own face into which he looked—the hair and its cut the same, the clothes duplicates of the ones he was wearing.

Turning, Mike jumped behind the wheel of the jeep, threw it into gear and gunned it toward the distant rocket. Reaching the gantry apron he braked in a swirl of sand. A guard stood by the elevator and Mike spoke with hard authority.

"Drive this back," he said, and stepped into the elevator cage.

At the top he ducked into the crowded passenger area just inside the rocket entrance. The bucket seats were each occupied except for the one beside Dr. Y Chi Tung.

The tiny Chinese physicist looked up solemnly as the lanky engineer approached, scanning his face intently. Then a twinkle came into his eyes to belie the still solemn expression.

"Confusion say," he declared softly, "that he who make big project is often center of many wheels."

Mike took the seat at which the other gestured, looked down at him speculatively, and started to answer. Then decided against it. *I am supposed to be dead now,* he thought; *and there is another man supposed to be here in my place. I do not know why, and I do not know what Ishie here knows. But this is not the place to ask questions.*

Then, in spite of himself, he asked grimly, "What could be expected to happen if the Big Wheel didn't spin out on time?"

"The Big Wheel?" Ishie's voice was still soft. "It is HOT ROD that is the key to the power—or the glory."

"Of course." Mike nodded, and neither spoke again until after blastoff. Even then, and during the long hours of flight to orbit, they spoke seldom and the subject was not referred to. The physicist sat quiet, seemingly undisturbed, beside him, as Mike tried to focus his mind away from the design and engineering factors which had for so long completely absorbed his attention, to contemplate the question of just why and to what end his murder had been attempted.

I

U. N. Space Lab I hung in its thirty-six hour orbit.

The huge wheel resembled nothing quite so much as a truck tire—mounted on a rim with rather oversize spokes and an undersize central hub—flung into the sky by man.

Around the wheel clustered its service units, each tethered and many at distances that would have been impractical if the setting had not been space: the atomic pile that powered the wheel and its satellite units, fourteen miles out along a slender thread; the "dump", a loosely-webbed conglomerate of individual units that had not yet been mounted; and the Hellmaker, Project HOT ROD—nearly five miles away on another slender thread—an experimental laser power station that was theoretically an independent operation, but that required the wheel's facilities for housing its personnel.

Making his way from square to square of the rope hairnet that served as guidelines on the outer surface of the Big Wheel, Mike Blackhawk, designer and chief engineer, completed his inspection of the gold-plated plastic hull with its alternate dark and shiny squares. He had scanned every foot of the curved surface in this first inspection, familiarizing himself with what other men had constructed from his drawings.

Now he let his eyes roam over the huge hull in satisfaction; then let his gaze leave the hull for the backdrop of space. He was shadowed from the sun at this spot, but the Earth hung over him—close, eye-filling, diminishing by its tremendous solidity his own flea-sized importance. Quickly he brought his gaze back to the hull on which he stood and the less minimizing perspective that it offered.

My buffalo looks good, he thought. Real good, he decided. He attached his safety line to a guideline leading to the south polar lock and kicked off, convinced that the lab itself was, at least so far, unharmed and ready for the job of turning on the spin with which he had planned to begin his three months' tour of duty out here. The laws of radiation exposure set the three month deadline to service aboard the lab, and he had timed his own tour aboard to start as the ship reached completion, ready for the delicate task of turning her on.

Many crews had come and gone in the eighteen months since the first payload had arrived at this orbit, but now the first of the scientists for whom the lab had been built were aboard; and the pick of the crews selected for the construction had been shuttled up for the final testing and spin-out.

Far off to his left and slightly below him a flicker of flame caught Mike's eye, and he realized without looking down that the retro-rockets of the shuttle on which he had arrived were slowly putting it out of orbit and tipping it over the edge of the long gravitic well that held Earth at its core. It would be two weeks before the shuttle returned.

Two weeks. And in that time he would have to find answers that weren't found by asking questions; and whether he lived or died—and possibly whether Lab I and HOT ROD lived or died as scientific projects—might hinge on those answers. But for now the job was to act as though nothing had happened; and to make sure that the Lab would spin without either man-made or accidental incident.

Nearing the lock he grasped the cable with one hand,

slowing himself, turned with skill and landed catlike on the stat-magnetic walk around the lock. He grinned inside his spacesuit. Like riding a bicycle, he thought. Your muscles remember the tricks of weightless motion.

He had gone over the inside of the wheel minutely before coming to its surface. Now there was only one more inspection before he turned on the spin. Around this south polar hub-lock, which would rotate with the wheel, was the stationary anchor ring on which both the stat-walk and the anchor tubes of the smaller units that served as distant components of the mother ship rode free. Kept rigid by air pressure, any deviation corrected by pressure tanks in the stationary ring, the tubes served both to keep the smaller bodies from drifting too close, and prevented their drifting off.

The anchor tubes were just over one foot in diameter, weighing less than five ounces to the yard—gray plastic fiber, air-rigid fingers pointing away into space—but they could take over 2,000 pounds of compression or tension, far more than needed for their job which was to cancel out the light drift motion caused by crews kicking in or out, or activities aboard. Uncancelled, these motions might have caused the baby satellites to come nudging against the space lab; or to scatter to the stars.

There had been talk of making the tubes larger so that they might also provide passageway for personnel without the necessity for suiting up; but as yet this had not been done. Perhaps later they would prove to have been the forerunners of space corridors in the growing complex that would inevitably develop around such a center of man's activities as this laboratory.

Mike's eyes followed the anchor tubes that centered him like the first strands of a spider's web: the far pile, shielded only by the vacuum of the space around it, conniving at its own banishment by powering the solar energy experiment that would render it obsolete; the dump, resembling nothing so much as a scattering of children's toys; and HOT ROD, the big, clear-fronted balloon that would focus the raging energy of the distant sun into pinpoint focus at Earth surface to provide power for a civilization.

HOT ROD. Mike's eyes narrowed as he looked down the long anchor tube to the balloon tethered as though against the stars.

HOT ROD packs the power, he thought; the power that, focussed on the cities of Earth could back up any demands made in its name. But to capture HOT ROD you'd need to replace more than one man aboard this satellite. But—how many have been replaced?

With a shake of his head he turned again to his job, and carefully checked the servo-motor that would maintain the stationary position of the ring around the hub with clocklike precision against the drag of bearing friction and the spin of the hub on which it was mounted. He briefly looked over the network of tubes before entering the air lock.

Inside, he stripped off the heavy, complicated armour of an articulated space suit, appearing in the comfortable shorts, T-shirt, and glove-leather, soft-soled slippers that were standard wear for all personnel.

He was lockering his suit as another figure entered from the air lock. He waited while the other shucked his suit with rather precise movements. A spare figure emerged, tall and rather old by ship's standards—late forties? Mike recognized him as either a scientist, or technician, named, of all things, Smith.

Mike grinned at him. "We're ready to roll the wheel!" he said exuberantly.

A thin smile answered him. "Congratulations," the other said, laconically.

Mike was undaunted. This wheel was his baby and it was ready to roll. At last. All the sweat and the swearing, all the impossible engineering obstacles and the impossibly stubborn materials; all the work and hope and dreams of man's first complete satellite base were in orbit, ready for spin-out. Nobody had stopped it yet, and spin-out it would.

He felt elated as a schoolboy as he dove down the central axial tube of the hub, past the personnel entrances from the rim, the entrances to the bridge and the gymnasium-shield area. He finally settled in the engineering quarters just below the north personnel entrances from the rim, and the observatory that occupied the north polar section of the hub.

The engineering quarters, like all the quarters of the hub, were thirty-two feet in diameter. Ignoring the ladder up the flat wall, Mike pushed out of the port in the central axis tunnel and dropped to the circular floor beside the power console. Strapping himself down in the console seat, he flipped the switch that would connect him with Systems Control Officer, Bessandra Khamar, at the console of the ship's big computer, acronymically known as the Sad Cow.

"Aiee-yiee, Bessie! It's Chief Blackhawk!" he whooped irreverently into the mike. "Ready to swing this buffalo!"

"Damn it, Mike! That's no way to use an official channel. If it hadn't been in a baby bottle, you'd have made me spill my coffee."

"Wait an hour, and your next cup of coffee you shall have, with proper gravity, in a cup instead of a baby bottle," Mike told her cheerfully. "Lab I's checked out ready to roll. Want to tell our preoccupied slipstick jockeys in the rim before we roll her, or just wait and see what happens? They shouldn't get too badly scrambled at one-half RPM—that's about .009 gee on the rim-deck—and I sort of like surprises."

"No you don't," Bessie said. "Anyhow, slipstick jockeys indeed! Your obsolescence is showing. Nobody's used a slipstick since the pocket computer was invented."

"It's a generic term that doesn't modernize," Mike said, unrepentant.

"Besides," her voice was severe, "you need captain's permission to roll the lab, our *scientific personnel* need an alert, and I need time to finish programming on the Sad Cow to be sure this thing doesn't wobble enough to shake us all apart. Even at a half RPM, your seams might not hold with a real wobble, and I don't like the idea of falling into a vacuum bottle as big as the one out there without a suit."

"Okay, so how much time will all that take?"

The speaker hummed off, and Mike waited almost two minutes before it came alive again.

"Captain's permission received, Mr. Blackhawk," came Bessie's formal voice. "We will have a thirty minute alert, and then you may start spin." There was another brief pause, and then Bessie's voice came formally over the all-stations annunciator system.

"Now hear this. Now hear this. All personnel. On my mark it is T minus thirty minutes to spin-out check. According to program, acceleration will begin at zero, and the rim is expected to reach .009 gee at one-half revolutions per minute in the first sixty seconds of operation. We will hold that spin until balance is complete, when the spin will slowly be raised to two revolutions per minute, giving .15 gee on the rim deck.

"All loose components and materials should be secured. All personnel are advised to suit up, strap down and hang on. We hope we won't shake anybody too much. Mark and counting."

Almost immediately on the announcement came another voice over the comm line. "Hold, hold, hold. We've got eighteen hundred pounds of milling equipment going down Number Two shaft to the machine shop, and we can't get it mounted in less than twenty minutes. Repeat, hold the countdown."

"The man who dreamed up the countdown was a Brain," Mike muttered over his open intercom for Bessie's benefit. "But the man who thought up the 'hold' was a damned genius."

"Holding the countdown." It was Bessie's official voice. "It is T minus thirty and holding. Why are you goons moving that stuff ahead of schedule and without notifying balance control? What do you think this is, a rock-bound coast? Think we're settled into bedrock like New York City? I should have known," she muttered, forgetting to switch off her connection to the engineering quarters. "My horoscope said this would be a shaky sort of day."

Blackhawk grinned to himself. Obviously, Bessie had not been replaced. Nobody could imitate her particular characteristics that well, he decided. But the rest of the bridge personnel?

With a quick glance at his console, which he'd keyed to standby for spin, he jumped to the opening to the central axis tunnel, kicked down the tunnel, and stuck his head in the bridge hatch.

The three bridge consoles—Command, Communications, and Computer—seemed to hang upside down in a circle around him, equispaced around what would be the floor when spin began. The captain's console was empty. Chad Clark at Communications, was busy murmuring

over a line plugged into the Earth channel, probably outlining the upcoming spin-out test for headquarters at U.N.
Project Space Lab Base, and for the news networks that
would be broadcasting the event. He had his hushmike
on, making it possible to keep up a running narration
without disturbing the rest of the bridge.

Mike scrutinized the man carefully. Yes, that was
Clark, he decided, noticing an abrupt gesture of the
hand. Even from above he could be sure.

He turned his attention to Bessie at the Computer,
busy with papers; then slid through the opening and took
the seat by her side. She looked up, startled.

"Is it really legal," he asked in mock severity, "to
use such a tremendously complicated chunk of equipment
as the Sacred Cow for casting horriblescopes? What's
mine today? Make it a good one and I won't report you
to U.N. Budget Control."

She smiled happily at him, the pert Eurasian features
beneath the shiny, cut-short straight black hair unabashed.
"Offhand," she told him, unrepentant, "I'd say today
was your day to be cautious, quiet and respectful to your
betters, namely me. However," she added in a conciliatory
tone, "since you put it on a Budget Control basis, I'll
ask the Cow to give you a real, mathematicked-out-plan-
ets-and-houses-properly-aligned, reading.

"Hey, Perk!" Her finger flipped the observatory com
line switch and the switch that would put a reply on the
console speaker instead of her ear phones. "Have you got
the planets lined up in your 'scopes yet? Where are they?
The Sacred Cow wants to know if they're all where they
ought to be?"

The speaker hummed alive, and Mike could almost
feel Dr. P.E.R. Kimball, PhD, FRAS, in his observatory,

forming a startled reply. When the answer came, though, it was cheerful, if puzzled.

"I did not realize that you would wish additional observational data before the swing began," the cheerfully meticulous voice answered. "Even though the observatory does not rotate with the wheel, I was told to expect a few wobbles as rotation was initiated, and have been putting my equipment in order for that potential, so I shan't be able to give you figures of any accuracy for some hours yet. Any reading I could give you now would be accurate only to within two minutes of arc—relatively valueless."

"Anything within half an hour of arc right now would be okay." Bessie's voice hid a grin.

"In that case, the astronomical data in the computer's memory should be more than sufficiently precise for your needs." There was a dry chuckle. "Horoscopes again?"

"Why are you baiting him?" Mike asked her curiously.

Bessie laughed as she began extracting figures from the computer's innards for a "plus or minus thirty seconds of arc" accuracy. "He's in charge of the observatory," she said lightly, "and he's a good sort."

He smiled, glancing casually at the figures she was extracting, then his eyes narrowed as he looked at them closely. Abruptly he pulled out a pen, picked up a pad of paper from the console, and began sketching rapidly. Then he spoke without looking up.

"These are angular readings from our present position," he said in an annoyed tone. "Get the Cow to rework them into a solar pattern."

"Yes, sir, Chief Blackhawk, sir. Your slightest wish. . . ." But Mike paid no attention to her sarcasm.

"And tell that Sacred Cow that you ride herd on to

give me a polar display pattern on one of the peepholes up there," he continued, indicating the thirty-six video screens above the console on which the computer could display practically any information that might be desired —including telescopic views, computational diagrams, or even the habitats of the fish swimming in the outer rim channels.

The display appeared in seconds on the main screen, and Mike growled as he saw it.

"Have the Cow advance that pattern two days," he said furiously. Then, as the new pattern emerged, "I should have known it. It looks as though we're being set up for a damned solar flare. Right when we're getting rolling. It might be a while, though. Plenty of time to check out a few gee swings. But best you rehearse your slipstick jockeys in emergency procedures."

"A flare, Mike? Are you sure?"

"Of course I'm not sure. But those planets sure make the conditions ripe. Look," and he laid his pencil across the screen as a straight line dividing the pattern neatly through the center.

"Look at the first six planets, all bunched on one side of the sun. Jupiter's right on the line. And Mercury won't be leaving until after Jupe crosses that line. Hadn't thought to check before, but that's about as predictable as anything the planets can tell you. We can expect a flare, and probably a dilly."

"Why, Mike? If a solar flare were due, U.N. Labs wouldn't have scheduled us this way. What makes you so sure that means there's a solar flare coming? I thought they weren't predictable?"

"It's new research, and they haven't got answers yet. But it's fairly old superstition," Mike said. "You play with horoscopes, but my people have been watching the stars and predicting since time began. When the planets line up on one side of the sun, you get trouble from man and beast and nature.

"It wasn't until magnetic storms began blanketing their radio waves that your slipstick boys got interested—a flare sure plays hell with communications equipment. But my people watched the interplay between the Earth and its creatures and the stars, and they worried about the seasons and how they felt and when the buffalo would get restless.

Yep, there's a flare coming. Whether it's caused by gravitational pull when you get the planets all to one side of Sol; or whether it's magnetic interaction between the bunched planetary fields and the field of the sun, I don't know. But I know it happens."

"Shucks," she said, "we had a five-planet line-up in 1967, I think it was, and nothing happened, nothing at all. The seers—come to think of it, some of them were Indians, but from India—the seers all predicted major catastrophes and the end of the world and all kinds of things, and nothing happened."

"Bessie," Mike's voice was serious, "I remember that year as well as you do. You had several factors that were different then—but you had solar flares then. Quite spectacular ones. You just weren't out here where they make a difference of life and death."

For an instant he saw the wheel in which he sat as the tiny, vulnerable bubble that it was, surrounded by the infinite majesty of space—a puny ring of plastic flung impudently toward the stars by infant hands. . . .

Then his jaw set. *Man's dreams are not puny,* he told himself grimly: *and not the scheming of all the subversives of Earth nor the smashing might of the entire solar furnace will stop us. . . .*

Aloud he spoke fiercely. "Don't let anybody or any-thing hold us too long getting this station lined up and counted down and tested out. Because we've got things building up out there, and we may get that flare, and it may not be two days coming." He pushed himself to a handhold on the edge of the central tunnel through the hub, and kicked on to the engineering quarters.

II

U.N. Space Lab I hung above a world scarred, scared and bickering—a symbol, for all its tiny fragility, of the search for the higher goals, for unity and for the freedom of the stars.

The questions symbolized in the fragile plastic wheel and its tethered adjuncts, visible from Earth as a slow-moving star, were now in debate in the halls of the U.N. —itself a tenuous structure of men and morals, attempt-ing to unite the civilizations it represented.

The question had been presented short years before in its most ruthless form: unite or die. It had been pre-sented as one small nation had attempted a world-jacking, holding the threat of atomic geneticide over the heads of another nation, and proving once and for all that tech-nological power is not a secret that can be hidden and contained.

The catastrophe had been brief and horrible, and two small nations had been wiped from the face of the Earth, not slowly in the attrition of the daily bombings to which mankind had adjusted his morals and ethics, but over-night in a holocaust that threatened to engulf the world.

Because the leaders of all nations forbore to join the conflict; because the major nations stood almost side by side in horror and attempted to halt the conflagration, renouncing for themselves the use of such weapons, civilization had survived—but it had been a chancy thing, that survival.

It had been human horror, then, that had forced the politics of disarmament. Overnight the U.N. was given the power to inspect any country or any manufacturing complex anywhere in the world—inspection privileges that overrode national boundaries and considerations of national integrity—and the U.N. Security Corps, a police force comprised of men from every nation, to back this up.

It had been a shotgun wedding, contrived in the face of a threat to survival, not grown from understandings. And now each nation, having given up its rights to bear arms, defended fiercely the right to retain its own individualistic freedoms.

As the bickerings grew, so grew the isolation of the resented men who enforced the peace; as the incidents grew, so grew the insolence with which the incidents were overcome. As the challenges to power came, so came the strengthening of the forces that must meet those challenges.

Recovering from the horror of the short holocaust, honest men debated in their hearts and in their halls of government, and brought the question to the U.N. floor —were the shackles they had imposed upon themselves those of the security that made freedom possible, or the security of slavery?

The arms of warfare had been foregone—but the battles of ideologies, the economic battles, the battles for leadership and supremacy went unabated.

Yet the world could no longer afford either the outright conflicts of ideologies, or the less apparent strangulation of economic control; and U.N. Security slowly assumed the role of policeman, not only for the seeking out and destruction of possible hoards of atomic weapons or the materials from which they could be assembled, but the muzzling of those who preached an ideology to their neighbors. And from that it was but a small step to the investigation of the economic controls by which one nation sought to take precedence over another.

No hard and fast rules could be drawn to distinguish between a casual remark made in one country as to one's own preference for one's own ideology and an active subversion designed to bring another country to one's own ideology. No hard and fast rules could be drawn to distinguish between an economic deal profitable to both sides, and a deal which would result in control. No hard and fast rules could be made to distinguish between raw materials or manufacturing potential designed for peaceful products, and those for atomic production.

So the activity of "subversion"—to be denounced and destroyed by U.N. Security forces—became a matter of definition; and the power to back up the definition lay only in the U.N., where debate raged endlessly; or more accurately, with U.N. Security, where action preceded debate.

Under those circumstances, armed forces of the most idealistic type could not but be found in error, whatever their actions. Under those circumstances, the human being in uniform—and the leaders of those human beings— were forced more and more into the role of overlord. There grew among these new overlords the feelings and certainty that the debates in the halls of government were those of a pack of children, each demanding protection from the other, each horrified that such discipline should apply to himself.

It was a situation that could not long endure, that must explode. And it was being debated—with more result than usual—in the halls of the U.N. as the governments of the world met to decide whether, in a reach for freedom, mankind had not made the first turn in the coil that would bind the mass of the many to the will of the few.

There were bills proposed and discussed in the Assembly that would loosen the ties by which man had bound himself to U.N. Security; and those bills would be up for vote within the week.

Yet beneath the restive bickering, in spite of the chafing controls that assured "peace in our time," the ties of the marriage that had begun as a shotgun wedding were beginning to forge. These ties were tenuous yet—the meetings of scientists and engineers, intermingling of peoples—more a tribute to the age of transportation and communication than to the fact of international arms control. Rather like a couple forced to sleep together in a double bed where, even though they quarrel, the strangeness, the animosities, the barriers tend to dissipate.

Of the ties that were forging, the most heartening was Space Lab I, hanging serene above an embittered world, a stepping-stone towards knowledge; a stepping-stone towards the freedom of the stars.

Bessie Khamar, sitting at the console of the Sad Cow waiting out the hold, began switching its smaller screens from section to section of the rim, and quietly wondered whether the tensions of the Earth were really focalized upon the absorbed personnel of the gigantic lab, or whether she had imagined that the lab could inspire such focalization.

Born of the generation that inherited a technology, she had faced from childhood, like her peers throughout the planet, the question of whether she would relax into the realms of jobs, entertainment, sports and the arts; or set herself to the hard disciplines demanded of those who preferred to understand and control the forces that were giving mankind a new freedom.

For the new freedoms were planet-wide, and were not a question of politics. They lay in the luxuries of electric power and mechanical transportation; of instant communications—the telephone, the TV, the radio; of washing machine and automatic furnace; of automated factory and farm.

The freedom of man lay at his fingertips. The only question in her mind was whether mankind could find his way to the economic and political freedoms that these automated servants made possible.

It was when she was introduced, first to cybernetics and then to the computer that she decided where her function lay.

People, she discovered, had behaviour reactions very similar to those of the automatons that had taken over the drudgery of civilization. As individuals, people would react in the manner of the time-binder, the thinker, man; but in statistical numbers they reacted as a computer—not in the logical patterns of thought, but in the pattern of reaction to whatever feedback was applied.

It became obvious that with a statistical group of people, the net result of action could be effectively vectored by one person in an obscure position utilizing selective feedback mechanisms on the group.

At one point she had unobtrusively, and for no other reason than to test her theory to her own satisfaction, fed the computer at the university she attended in such a way that one whole area of the university program was re-oriented to a new pattern of learning that gave key to the individual as versus the mass. The ease with which her goal had been accomplished without anyone noticing that they were being maneuvered, the pinpoint accuracy with which she had been able to achieve an exactly specified goal, both impressed and terrified her.

Thereafter she devoted the vitality and energy that the majority of her peers were throwing into confrontations with the establishments of their various civilizations, to a study of the complex computer network that under-lay those establishments and their functionings and to an understanding of the vectors being applied and the reactions that could be predicted.

Quietly Bessie put most of her attention on the cybernetic patterns by which man responded to his civilization and the programming that directed it, while on the surface she simply made herself one of the most skillful of computer programmers. And constantly she fed into whatever computer was under her fingers the factors of a civilization learning to be interdependent, seeking predictions of the crucial points, the points at which the forces melding the nations could be vectored towards freedom for the individual.

By the time that her studies and predictions indicated with high probability that the question of individual freedom as versus the state would focalize in Space Lab I, she was in a position to use the computers that were her tools to get herself aboard the big wheel at the indicated time of crisis.

It was necessary that she remain unobtrusive as a

person—but she need make no real effort in that direction. No one looked behind a computer console for more than simple efficiency in programming.

Yet, under the fingers of computer operators lay the vast network that fed the answers to men's questions—answers on which almost all decisions were based in the business, industrial and military decision-making areas. Under their fingers lay the slanting of the information that would be played into memory banks to dictate the content of those answers. Under their fingers lay the networks of circuits that handled automated machinery, the content of messages and orders from one spot to another; the propaganda mills. They truly directed the technology that had been developed to electronic speeds and that could not be supervised or ordered other than electronically, for man's thinking mind and "reasoned" reactions were far too slow to handle the instantaneous actions of the equipment he had developed and built.

The Cow sat quiet, seemingly inert, before her but in its innards, she knew, impulses were constantly flowing, orders were being given and changed, micromeasurements made and microreactions ordered. The entire ship was operated and controlled by the myriad systems programmed into the Cow and handled by its circuits. The air, the waters, the life support systems, the flow of power, the balance of the wheel, its relationships with its subsidiary units, and with the peoples aboard—all were monitored and balanced in a constant flow of measurement and change, of action and dictated reaction.

Dissecting the Cow's operations and its knowhow would have been an undertaking that few engineers would even attempt. One of the first major computers, back in the early '60s, had made that fact abundantly clear. It had been given a circuit to simplify, and when the simplification was complete, it had been given the simplified circuit to simplify. After five such simplifications the engineers had put the resultant circuit to work—and it had worked well and efficiently—but when they tried to analyze the principles on which it functioned, they had been unable to deduce them.

That the computer complex was basic to a technological civilization, most people recognized. The extent to which their programming influenced that civilization, a very few had noted.

But, the real potential of the computer, so far as Bessie knew, had not even been guessed—the potential that lay in the interconnections of the computer systems of the planet.

The Cow before her constantly fed information to, and was fed information by data lines that led into the complex of scientific data-gathering computers—data lines that led into the heart of the military networks of computers; data lines that led into the banking and marketing and manufacturing and weather networks, and into the centralized information-gathering and storage banks.

And each of the computer complexes into which the Cow fed and by which she was fed had interconnections throughout the other complexes, until the entire planet could be seen to be webbed by a system that could, properly programmed, be united into one operating whole. For each data line was capable of carrying programming, and the system by which computer programmed computer had long since been developed.

The potential existed, quiescent, within the electronic network that handled the planet's automaticities. To use that potential would be a drastic action. To justify the use of such a potential, a crisis must equate to the question of permanent freedom or slavery for the entire planet.

Would the crisis now building on Earth reach those proportions she wondered? Would the measures now being debated on the U.N. floor bring on such a crisis when they were brought to vote?

Bessie did not know. She doubted that many people so much as guessed at the possibility.

She looked up to see that Captain Naylor Andersen had arrived while she was preoccupied, and was seated at his console. How long had he been there? Had he heard what Mike said? Probably, she decided.

"Put the remote control video on my console screens, too," the captain ordered briefly. His huge frame was relaxed into his chair. He pulled the stump of a well-chewed cigar from his pocket and clamped it, unlit, between his lips, watching the pre-spin activities on the rim, but making no comment when he found the order to suit-up being ignored.

Whether Nails Andersen was more politician or scientist it would be hard to say, Bessie thought. Certainly his rise through the ranks of U.N. Bureaus had been rapid. Certainly in this rise he had been political, with the new brand of politics that men were assaying—world, rather than national. Certainly, also, he was a scientist, and he had used his political abilities in behalf of science, pushing and slashing at red tape barriers.

More than most, he was responsible for the existence of Space Lab I and HOT ROD. How would he line up in the coming political battles?

She didn't know. Space was his dream, his frontier, his goal; but how, in the bickerings of men, he might consider it would be best achieved—that was a question to which he'd given, at least to his crew, no clue.

The video scenes flickered silently on both consoles. In Rim Sector A-9—the Biological Laboratory—Dr. Claude Lavalle appeared to be having his troubles. He obviously wasn't going to take time to suit up. Bessie smiled gently. Dr. Lavalle was neither spaceman nor politician—just a damned good biologist.

Claude Lavalle had originally planned to leave his stock of animals, which contained sets of a great many of the species of the small animals of Earth, on their own gravity-bound planet until well after the spin supplied a modicum of gravity to the ship; but the shuttle schedule had proved such as to make possible the trip either far in the future, or to put him aboard on this trip, with spin only a few hours away.

The cages with their loads of guinea pigs, rabbits, hamsters and other live animals to be used in the sacrificial rites of biochemical research could not be allowed to become a mess, for any mess would be free-floating in the sealed containers and quite possibly fatal as it was breathed in by the animals. The time of free-fall had been sufficiently short that no provision had to be made for feeding or watering under those conditions, but constant air filtering was a necessity, and the filters must be cleaned with the utmost rapidity.

The biologist was much too busy to take time to suit up, and was wishing fervently that his assistants could have been sent up on the shuttle with him.

The screen flickered. In Rim Sector A-10, the FARM— Fluid Agricultural Recirculating Method Control Lab—

Dr. Millie Williams, her satiny brown skin contrasting with her white T-shirt and shorts, also looked to be having her troubles, and also showed no signs of suiting up. Would the captain pull protocol and insist, Bessie wondered? It wasn't really necessary, and he'd made no move to do so. . . .

The trays of plants in the FARM, in beds of sponge plastic and hydroponic materials, were all sealed against free-fall, but Millie Williams was hastily orienting them for the pseudo-gravity of the coming rotational spin. The vats of plankton and algae concentrates were not so important as to orientation, she knew, but she also knew that they should be fed into their rim-river homes as soon as possible, though this could not be done until the rim-spin was well under control.

At present the ship's personnel was existing almost entirely on imported, tanked air; imported, concentrated foods. If the ARK and the FARM came through as scheduled, the Wheel should be handling its own air and food supplies within two weeks—a closed, self-sufficient ecology. If they failed in that—well, air purification and waste recycling might become possible from the work of Dr. Carmencita Schorlemmer in the Chem Lab; or Dr. Y Chi Tung, that unimposing though eminent physicist might get around to finishing his work in air restoration by gas dialysis membranes. . . .

The captain flipped a screen to the dump outside where it picked up a duo of ordinary spacemen—which meant that they had only a little more specialized training than the average PhD. Paul Chernov and Tombu M'Numba? Bessie couldn't be sure through their spacesuits, but she rather thought so.

Paul Chernov was fine-boned, blond, with an ancestral background of the Polish aristocracy; Tombu a black, muscular giant—a Swahili, minor king of a minor country, but an aristocracy that extended far behind the comparable lines for any European aristocracy. Tombu himself counted his kingdom in negative terms, terms that were no longer applicable in his mind to a modern world.

It was an odd combination, Bessie thought—one of the strangest even of this multinational spaceship, for the two worked well together and had become by nature inseparable. Yet even odder was the fact that, against their herited backgrounds, each had become a top machinist, that in each, youth and vitality were directed with an insatiable thirst towards the technological knowledge that were demanded by space. . . .

Paul Chernov twisted and turned with a practised ease that was his pride and delight as he searched the conglomeration of floating objects tethered to the Dump's anchor tube for the ECM lathe he was after. Finally, looking almost directly along the eastern bulge of the African coast "below" him, he sighted what was probably the lathe, and kicked himself towards it. Simultaneously he pulled his Rate of Approach Indicator from the socket on his suit.

The RAI gun, he sometimes felt, was the real reason he'd become a spaceman in these tame days. Even if he couldn't be a space pirate, it gave him the feel.

Humming to himself, he aimed the search beam from the tiny gallium-arsenide laser crystal that was the heart of the gun at the bulky object he sought, and read off the dial at the back of the gun barrel the two meter/second approach velocity and the twenty-eight meter distance. He could as easily have set the RAI gun to read his velocity and distance in centimeters or kilometers; and it would have read as well his rate of retreat, if that had been the factor.

Paul's RAI gun might be, to others, a highly refined, vastly superior great-grandson of the older radar that had required much more in the way of equipment than the tiny bulk of this device, but to him, alone in his spacesuit, it was the weapon with which he conquered the stars.

In the distance, off beyond the wheel in its trailing orbit, the huge spherical shape of HOT ROD glowed its characteristic green—another application of the laser principle, but macroscopic in comparison to the tiny laser rate-of-approach gun.

Happily, Paul burst into song.

> *I studied and worked and learned my trade*
> *I had the life of an Earthman made;.*
> *But I met a Spacer and I got waylaid—*
> *And I'm here where I wasn't going. . . .*

From the far side of the dump Tombu's voice bellowed into his ears over the intercom. "If you have to sing, cut down the volume."

Paul grinned and reached for the volume control.

"Okay, okay! Heave a line over this way and let's get this ECM lathe aboard."

"Maybe we'd best wait 'till spin's on. The countdown's started."

"Hell, there's already a 'hold.' Might be next week before she spins. Let's get the lathe lashed down and up to the stat-walk, then we can query Balance Control."

Tombu laughed, his deep voice hearty even over the lowered volume. "Balance Control, Budget Control, Security Control—I'll be glad when the new bills get voted through. I've already got a job with an Independent where we can be spacemen instead of Security minions."

"An intercom's open to anybody," Paul cautioned sharply.

"And anybody that wants to can listen to my sentiments." Tombu was making his way across the Dump to meet Paul at the lathe. "The bill will be through in a few weeks. Everybody knows it's going to pass, and that anybody that wants to can go to space then. Anyhow, calling space a half-step-forward, three-steps-back Security stronghold isn't talking ideologies. It's talking fact."

Paul grinned. Even if anybody were listening it probably didn't matter, although his tendency was to keep his conversation safe and secure. Almost in defiance of his own tendencies, he said aloud, "It'll sure be great to have the whole thing opened up again. Damned if I like Big Brother breathing down my neck every move I make."

Tombu was trying to attach a line to the bulky lathe, which slipped away and away from his efforts until he finally got it to the end of its tether where it would strain against that instead of floating obstinately away from any touch.

"What'll we do if the bill doesn't go through?" he asked fiercely. "How long do you suppose the space program will last if Security stays in the saddle?"

"At its present pace—years and years, but we'll still be playing with rockets, and all the real know-how we've got on true space drives will be buried, along with their designers."

"Yeah. Are we going to put up with that?"

"Hell, the bill will pass. You put me up for a berth with that Independent, I hope?"

"Of course. But they can't announce anything until it's legal. I'll tell you about it, another time. But suppose the bill didn't pass?"

"Well, suppose it doesn't? What'll we do then?"

Tombu twisted in freefall, looked down at the big planet swinging slowly below them, then glanced at the balloon that hung, luminescently green, against the stars. He reached out and caught Paul's arm, drew his own RAI gun, and silently pointed it at HOT ROD.

"That's what we'll do," he said softly, aiming as though to fire a real gun. "That's what we'd have to do."

The silent video picture flipped, leaving Bessie wondering what the interplay had been about as the two space-suited figures had turned to look at the big balloon.

This time it was Rim Sector B-7—Security Headquarters. Major Steve Elbertson's Security corpsmen were suited up, some of them strapped down, some entering and leaving, evidently replacing unsuited men at other posts. Of course, she thought wryly. To a soldier an order's an order. Major Elbertson himself was probably in his small private office to the side.

One of the HOT ROD technicians—Smith?—was entering just as the captain, with an abrupt gesture, flipped off the video.

Bessie smiled to herself. That, she thought, tells me how our captain feels about Security—but his politics will not necessarily follow his personal feelings. . . .

Lathe Smith entered Security headquarters and headed straight for the small cubicle where Major Elbertson had his formal office.

An adjutant, seated at a desk just outside the C.O.'s office, was dressed, as were all the guards in the room, in full space rig except for the helmet, which was open. The civilian smiled his amusement thinly.

"Aren't you taking this spin-out rather seriously, Corporal?"

The adjutant looked up. "Mr. Smith," he said, "why are you not in your space suit?"

"I am not a member of Security, Corporal, and not subject to such orders."

"The orders are from the captain of the ship. You are a member of the ship's personnel, even as a technician of the scientific complement."

"I take the captain's . . . suggestion . . . as it was intended, an excuse for the timid. Technician Lathe Smith to see Major Elbertson," he ended formally, switching the subject.

The adjutant looked at him a moment with narrowed eyes. Then: "Major Elbertson is expected shortly. Please be seated."

Disregarding the last, Lathe wandered to one of the narrow portholes that looked into the fluorescently lighted rim rivers. This river was empty of life yet, but would soon be a seaquarium of unusual properties. How very much too bad, he thought, that Budget Control had insisted on the opaque walls in the various rim sections, rather than clear plastic that would have panelled each office and laboratory with seascapes. Surely the aesthetics of life aboard the satellite should have received some consideration. Though Budget Control, as he was in a position to know very well, was under the hidden but very firm hand of Security, and Security had few aesthetic properties in its makeup.

"The price one pays," he thought bitterly. "Once this brief skirmish is over, once man is assured unity under his natural leaders, such austere measures will no longer be necessary—or permitted. Then one can return to one's own title, leaving the 'technician' to underlings."

The title "technician"—and the attitudes engendered by the title—galled him more than he cared to admit even to himself. When they address the *Herr Doktor,* there will be no references to orders, from Captain Andersen or anyone else. He suppressed a tendency to plan a fitting revenge for the adjutant for the insubordination with which he had unwittingly spoken.

He felt, rather than heard, Steve Elbertson enter; felt it by the electric tension that preceded the man. Deliberately he kept his back to the room, his attention on the porthole.

"Smith!"

He turned slowly, casually.

"The Major will see you in his office."

Elbertson, space-suited but helmet open, was seated at his desk, and neither looked up nor rose until the door was firmly closed behind the visitor. Then his head snapped up, his nod, though brief, was cordial, and he half-rose as he spoke softly.

"Herr Doktor."

"Major." Smith seated himself without being asked in the chair by the corner of the Security officer's desk. Without preliminary he delivered his news. "Blackhawk himself is aboard."

The Major nodded. "There was a slip-up, if so inexpressive a term may be used in the face of what was actually a serious blunder. I do not know the details."

"Does this mean a postponement of our plans? It would be most unwise——"

The interruption was fierce. "Our plans do not permit a postponement. The melon is ripe *now*. No. I expect details of revised plans any moment now. Clark is on the lab communications board, and there should be no difficulty in the transmission of orders from Earth. It was most incautious of you to come here."

"I felt it necessary. I had seen Blackhawk and wanted to report the situation to you. It was possible that word of the failure to keep our man aboard and in charge had not reached you. I suppose our man is gone?"

The major nodded. "The timing was too abrupt to make it possible to keep him aboard. We have seen to it that the rotation rules are strict. We could have abrogated them in the face of the 'emergency' we had prepared; but to abrogate them without such an emergency might have tipped our hand."

A knock at the door interrupted them, and Steve Elbertson drew himself into formal attitude as his adjutant came in, returned the man's salute with studied carelessness.

The adjutant laid a carefully folded sheet of paper before the officer, saluted, motioned as though to click his heels—an obvious impossibility in his space armour—and left. The door closed behind him.

Smith waited quietly while the major read through the paper, then perused it once more, carefully.

"It's the communication I expected," he said finally. He leaned back in his chair and laid his gauntleted hands on the desk, glancing down at the paper, then back at the scientist.

"The plans are to remain as before. Two days after HOT ROD'S test, we will take over command of the complex and will secure the scientific personnel and such of the crew as refuse to cooperate. They will be 'detained' where there is no possibility of any communication with them. We will then, speaking with their voices—specifically with the voices of Captain Andersen, Dr. Koblensky and Blackhawk—do exactly what some idiot is bound to do if space is allowed to become open to every jackhead nation on the planet. It will be declared that 'we' are the first space people, that as such 'we' are a cut above anybody on Earth, and that 'we' hereby take over the space program from the United Nations Council. 'We' will declare that 'we' have overcome the Security forces aboard and are holding them prisoner.

"The U.N. Council will of course go into special session to decide what to do about the 'mad scientists' who have taken control of Lab One. That part is all set. The Council will ask for the 'scientist's' demands. The demands will be outrageous—that Earth is to produce and ship supplies, material, equipment et al to her 'space people' that will enlarge the program and the complex in the style that they would like to see—but which would practically bankrupt Earth.

"The communiques will point out that Earth is hostage. Three days later the 'mad scientists' will use HOT ROD to burn a small, nearly-uninhabited island to prove the point. HOT ROD will then be focused on each of the major cities in turn, the 'scientists' noting as each passes beneath the focus that that city *could* have been a target.

"The Council will vote full war powers to Security. As soon as Security is firmly in the saddle the real we—the Security Corps aboard the Lab—will 'escape' and 're-take' the wheel and the weapon.

"Since you are one of the Satellite's scientists—are not even known to be aboard in your own identity—you will, of course, not be implicated. Announcements on Earth will reveal that some form of space madness induced by radiation had affected the scientists. Earth will be told that, in their madness, they had taken control of the Laboratory and HOT ROD, and that the Security Corpsmen aboard had been captured in a surprise attack and were prisoners. That will remain the story while Earth Security consolidates the position and power to protect Earth after its first 'space attack.' Our people are placed. The stampede to Security is prepared, and the plan cannot be delayed. The time is ripe now.

"Our orders are to get rid of Blackhawk, preferably immediately after the HOT ROD test. Whether this can be accomplished in time to give Earth Security the excuse for sending up his 'assistant' on the shuttle is immaterial. They will send our man back up, with or without an excuse. Sufficient coverup can be handled on Earth.

"Our orders are not to wait for the replacement engineer, but to take the chance that the laboratory can operate without a chief engineer's services for the necessary period of time."

Smith nodded slowly. "Blackhawk will have an . . . accident, then?"

The Major smiled grimly. "Accidents in space are readily explicable."

"You are going to have a rather large number of 'accidents' to explain, after the fact, you know. There are 163 persons aboard Lab One and HOT ROD now. Except for the very highest echelon of those who will be in command, it will not be possible to be . . . secure in your story if too many of these are at large."

Elbertson shoved back his chair with a gesture of annoyance. "Amateurs at military strategy should stick to the scientific problems involved in their own work," he said curtly. Then: "Forgive me, Herr Doktor. My nerves are taut. You have every right to question whether our measures will be sufficient for the necessary take-over itself, and for the protection of all our reputations after that takeover." He paused, and the pause lengthened, but Smith's eyes did not waver from his face.

"The . . . personnel aboard—'mad scientists' you know—will be given the most considerate care at a Chilean hospital high in the Andes mountains where work in the mental effects of radiation exposure has long since been publicized as having achieved some spectacular results. The minor technicians and ordinary spacemen will recover rapidly, and will be assigned to posts in Antarctica and in underseas exploration."

"What about your own men? They drink, and they talk. I assume——"

"They are quite loyal, and they do their drinking and their talking among themselves. Any who behave otherwise have long been weeded out. However," and here the grim smile made itself apparent on his features, "there will be a need for guards at the hospital, of course."

Lathe Smith inclined his head courteously. Then he smiled his thin-lipped smile. "You have been quite thorough in your planning, and I must not take up too much of your time. However, if you will indulge me, there is one more detail with which I should like to familiarize myself. During the period when I am in charge of HOT ROD, and the ultimatum has been issued—theoretically by the 'mad scientists'—just how is this to be handled?"

"Oh, that." Elbertson picked up a pencil, found it awkward through his space suit gloves, laid it down again. "We shall be in control from the first, of course. The rest is a story—a movie, actually. It has long since been made, and is ready to play over the TV networks of Earth. While publicity films were being prepared, we were careful to include all the necessary shots we would need for such a film, and it has been quite simple, I am told, to piece them together into the necessary form. As for the voices —they are genuinely the supposed speakers' own.

"Doctoring tapes so that a given voice can be made to say anything you desire it to say has long since become a fine art. The experts can take a word here and a phrase there from anybody's taped speech and put them together on a new tape to form any sentences they like. It is quite remarkable.

"I have seen the . . . movie. It is chaotic in its form, and infinitely precise in the results to be achieved. Actually, it would make a box-office smash if it were a commercial venture. The realism! The heroics, when Security finally wins in the end and saves Earth from the threat. . . ." He paused, then quite suddenly his voice acquired a near snarl.

"If the human race per se had two brain cells to rub against each other, they would know that space is far too dangerous to be tackled by any Tom, Dick or Harry of a nation or corporation that can put together a drive-unit! How in the name of all that's holy do they expect to survive on a sitting-duck planet if any uncontrolled damnfool that can get to the asteroid belt were allowed to get there? All he'd have to do to be king-pin would be put a drive on an asteroid and head it in toward Earth. Just how long would civilization last if just *anyone* could issue an ultimatum and back it up with that kind of power? Do you have any idea what sort of weapon just one small—say a mile-long—nickel-steel asteroid, equipped with the most primitive of drives would represent? Why the hellmaker isn't in it for that kind of. . . ."

Smith's voice was dry. "I happen to be the scientist who pointed that fact out to your superiors some two years ago," he noted. Then, watching the man before him deflate, he added in a cutting voice, "And just what assurance do I have—and I think it had better be very concrete assurance, *General* Elbertson—that I will not be listed as one of the 'mad scientists' after I have done your little job for you, and find myself in a hospital in the Chilean Andes?"

Elbertson looked up, surprised. The surprise was unusual, and, Smith decided, genuine. "Why . . . you're dependent on us and we're dependent on you. That is the only real basis for trust between individuals, isn't it?"

Smith nodded slowly, but his voice lost none of its edge as he continued, his words paced so that each stood out distinctly from the others: "It is perhaps, then, quite unnecessary to point out that there are probably only two scientists alive today who are capable of handling HOT ROD's design and repair if fallacies should develop; and that Dr. Koblensky, who *will* be in your hospital, and who would refuse, in any case, to do your bidding, is the other one."

T minus three and counting.

On the zero signal Mike, in the engineer's quarters, would change the now idly-bubbling air jets in the rim rivers over to the fully-directional drive jets necessary to spin the fluid in counter-rotation through the rim tanks.

The suiting up and strapping down were probably unnecessary, Bessie thought from inside her own suit, donned when, as the 'hold' was released, the captain had personally ordered it for all aboard. But perhaps he's right, she thought. In space you don't take chances.

"T minus two and counting." Her own voice sounded official and clipped over the intercom.

From the physics lab came a rather oddly-pitched echo. "Hold it, please! Paul forgot to secure the electrolite for

42

the ECM equipment. Can not have five-gallon jugs bouncing around!"

"And we can't have you bouncing around either, Dr. Chi," came the captain's voice. "Get that soup under wraps quick. How much time do you need?"

Chad Clark's voice was just audible, murmuring over his Earth-contact phone. "There has been a hold. T minus two and holding. . . ."

Less than two minutes later, Dr. Chi released the hold by announcing briefly, "Machine shop and physics department secure."

"T minus two and counting. . . ." "T minus one and counting. . . ." Bessie continued officially. "Fifty, forty, thirty, twenty . . ."

The faint whine of high-speed centrifugal compressors could be heard through the ship.

"Ten . . ." The jets that had previously bubbled almost inaudibly took on the sound of a percolating coffee pot.

". . . four, three, two, one, mark."

The bubbling became a hiss that settled into a soft susurrus of background noise as the jets forced air through the rivers of water in the circular tanks of the rim. The water began to move. By reaction, the wheel took up a slow, circular motion in the opposite direction.

Then, gently, the wheel shook itself and settled into a complacently off-center motion that placed Bessie somewhere near the actual center of rotation.

"We're out of balance, Mr. Blackhawk," said the captain, one hand on the intercom switch.

"Bessie, ask the Cow what's off balance." It was Mike's voice from engineering control. "Thought we had this thing trued up like a watch."

But the computer had already taken over and was controlling the flow of water to the hydrostatic balance tank system, feeding water into one, drawing it from another in reducing increments as she oriented the axis of spin against the true axis of the wheel.

The wobble became a wiggle; the wiggle became the slightest of sways; and under the computer's gentle ministrations, the sways disappeared and Space Lab I rolled true.

Slowly Mike inched up the power of the jets, and the speed and "gravity" of the rim rose—from 0.009 to 0.039; to the pre-scheduled 0.15 of a gravity, two RPM, at which she would remain until a thorough test scheduled over several days had been accomplished. Later tests would put the rim through check-outs to as high as 1.59 gee, but "normal" operation had been fixed at two RPM.

In the background, the susurrus of the air jets rose slightly to the soft lullaby-sound that the wheel would always sing as she rolled.

III

New, experimental, her full complement of six hundred scientists and service personnel so far represented by only one hundred sixty-three aboard, the big wheel that was Space Lab I rotated majestically at her hydrodynamically controlled two revolutions per minute—more than half of her mass that of the waters that spun her.

Spun her? The deep rivers of water that surrounded the laboratories of the rim served almost as many purposes for the life within those laboratories as had the first warm waters of Earth in which life had come into existence. For man, who had evolved from the amoebae that formed and grew in the seas of the planet, had found that he must take a part of the mother waters with him when he sought the stars, if he were to survive the search.

The huge rivers that formed the shell of the rim held the laboratories as in a tube through their center, forming a six foot shield between the fragile living things within and the fierce radiations of space.

Yet this was only one of the simpler of their functions. As a heat sink, the waters provided stability of temperature in space where no atmosphere intervened and the violence of heat on the sunside was only matched by the frigidity of the cold on the dark side.

As a method for controlling and changing the rate of rotation of the wheel, the rivers of water served as no other medium could; and as a means of static balancing, masses or microbits of water could be stopped and held in counterbalance tanks around the rim to compensate for the movements of men or machinery.

In effect, the entire ship operated against a zero-moment-of-inertia calculation which could be handled effectively only by the computer. The moment of inertia of the ship must be constantly calculated against the moment of inertia of the hydraulic mass flowing in the rim, and the individual counterbalance tanks must shift their loads so that stability was maintained.

The Cow's continuously operating feedback monitor system was capable of maintaining accuracy of balance to better than .01% in the mass inertial field of centrifugal forces, and while such extremely fine control might not be absolutely necessary to the individual comfort of the personnel aboard, it was very necessary to the accuracy of scientific observation, one major purpose of the lab. Even so, many of the experimenters would require continuous monitor information from the computer to correct their observations against her instantaneous error curve.

The rivers, too, served as biological cultural mediums, and were the basis for both air restoration and food supplies. It was because of these purposes that the water did not run as a single river, but was divided into twenty separate streams in each of which various biological reactions could be set up.

While a few of the rivers were in a nearly chemically pure state, most of them were already filling with the plankton and algae that had been brought aboard, and that would form the base of the major ecological experiments, some with fresh water as their medium, others using sea water complete with its normal micro-organisms. As the air jets that gave the ship its spin bubbled through these rivers, the algae and plankton and other growths would give that air back its oxygen in a natural manner that would obviate the necessity for the tanked oxygen on which the ship now survived.

Several of the rivers were operating to provide fish and other marine delicacies as part of the experiment to determine the best ways of converting algae to food in palatable form. Others were operating on different cycles to convert human waste to usable form so that it might reenter the cycles of food and air.

Within, the rivers were lighted fluorescently—an apparent anomaly that was due to the fact that direct sunlight out here would be far too fierce to be allowed to impinge on so shallow a medium.

This ecological maze of rivers and eddies and balance tanks; of air jets and currents and micro life; of spin-rate-control and shielding that formed the major portion of

Space Lab I, was all keyed to a servo-regulated interdependence that for this self-contained world replaced the stability achieved in planetary ecologies by the vastness of the planetary crust and atmosphere and waters.

Sitting in complacent control of these overall complexities that must be met with automatic accuracy was the Starrett Analogue/Digital Computer, Optical Wave Type 44-63, irreverently known as Sad Cow.

Space Lab I had been in spin for two days.

On Earth, TV viewers no longer demanded unending hours of Lab newscasts, and were returning to their normal daytime fare, which seemed far more exciting than the pictures of the interminably spinning wheel or the interviews with the scientists aboard that had filled their screens during the spin-out trial period.

On the wheel itself, life was settling into a pattern. The birds and beasts of the biological lab had adjusted to light gravity and tended to display disrupting agilities impossible on Earth. The plants in the FARM stretched themselves, jack-and-the-beanstalk style, towards the overhead fluorescents. The instruments in the observatory were returning vast reams of new data to Earth for analysis. The guards in Security had gotten over their awe of Space Service and settled into the grumbling that marks the "good" soldier.

And in the engineering quarters Mike was, somewhat cautiously, attempting to extract a bit of personalized, non-engineering type information from the Cow.

It was not the Chief Engineer's job to be in constant contact with the complete situation of the ship and its vast complexities, he well knew. Nor was it in the manuals that he should have access to the computer's huge memory banks and abilities other than through "channels"—i.e.,

Bessie. But the book definition of the information he needed for his job, and his own criteria, were somewhat different, so he had built on Earth and installed shortly after he came aboard, a subcontrol link which put him in direct contact with the placid Cow.

His original intention in rigging the link had been to use the calculator for that occasional math problem which might be more quickly resolved with her help; but then the criteria of needed information, or curiosity, or both, got the better of him, and the secret panel hidden in the legitimate control panels of an engineer's console was actually quite a complete link, covering all of the Cow's multiple functions without interfering in any way with Bessie's control links, or revealing its existence. This linkage gave Mike the only direct access to the computer's store of information and abilities other than the formal ones at the computer control console.

Mike's secret pride was the vocoder circuit with which he had terminated his link, originated because a teletype system similar to that used at the control console would have been too obvious, as well as because his normally nimble fingers tended to get tangled up on a keyboard.

Bessie and her assistants might speak to the Cow through the teletype link and switches at her control console, but only Mike had the distinction of being able to speak directly to the big computer, and get her complacent, somewhat moo-ing answers. And only Mike knew of the existence of the vocoder aboard. It would take some care to get used to the literal-minded conversation that resulted, Mike felt, but eventually he hoped to work out a satisfactory communications ability with the overtly obvious Cow.

What he wanted now was an estimate of the "situation" as it concerned himself, HOT ROD, the political unrest of Earth, and a prediction as to the potentials involved. If anyone—or anything, he corrected himself— could give him an unbiased analysis of the problem, the Sad Cow could do it.

He took some time figuring the content of the first question. Better lead into the subject slowly, he decided.

"Just how critical is the situation in respect to the control of the United Nations on Earth?" he asked finally, as an opener.

The Cow's mooing voice responded without inflection. "There are 4.177654 times ten to the ninth plus individual political entities concerned with the political situation on Earth, representing 4.177654 times ten to the ninth plus individual variants, of which an indeterminate number is actively concerned. . . ."

That could go on for hours, Mike decided. He interrupted. "Okay. Enough on that. In other words, you can't say exactly. Then, what political faction would be most likely interested in taking over control of Space Lab I immediately?"

And the complacent, "A priority listing would include every nation, as well as the allied groups of nations as. . . ."

"Okay. Enough." His questions were too general, Mike decided. Perhaps something more specific . . . ?

"Somebody, in an obviously well-organized manner, tried to murder me on my way to the shuttle. They had a replacement ready to take over my job. Who would have organized such an attempt?"

"Such an attempt would logically have been organized by someone who wanted a person other than yourself aboard in your place." The voice didn't even sound distressed, which, unreasonably, annoyed Mike as much as the answer.

"But how on Earth could they have hidden the difference of identity?"

"Such a difference in identity would be relatively simple to disguise on Earth," the mooing voice answered. "Among 4.177654 times ten to the ninth plus individuals. . . ."

"Damn." Mike was exasperated. "I mean . . . I meant. . . ." Then it dawned on him. The person who replaced him needn't actually be the engineer they wanted in charge. The double factors of resemblance and engineering ability would have been a little too much to attempt in one move, anyhow. The "double" could have gotten "sick" the moment he was aboard and been put in sick bay, where he'd remain unseen and unrecognized, while "their" man took over the engineering. Now—who would be the engineer aboard ready, capable, and in line to take over the job?

Obviously, the assistant who was already aboard, scheduled to be rotated back to Earth, but who could have been retained in the "emergency," Mike decided. With a sigh of relief he realized that at least he'd fouled them up on that score. The "replacement" was Earthside now, and they'd play hell trying to get him back again in under ninety days; or at least the two weeks until the shuttle returned.

So what would be the potential for any renewed excitement until their man could be returned? Well, to *that* the Cow could probably give him a reasonable answer.

"Could Space Lab I be handled without my presence aboard, or without a person of my competence?" he asked.

"The ship's computer is in charge and capable of handling any exigencies that could be expected to arise in the operation of Space Lab I." The complacent voice didn't change tone, but to Mike it sounded so self-satisfied that he was tempted to take a wrench to its insides.

"Never mind," he said, reaching for the switch-off key.

"Does that order include only your requests, or shall it be taped to include those from Control Center——"

"Cancel that order to 'never mind!' " Mike started to follow this with another remark, clamped his mouth shut, and switched off the vocoder. He found he was sweating.

The Cow activated by a chance remark, could probably wreak more havoc in microseconds than a roomful of subversives given a year, he thought.

Then he leaned back in relief. The Cow to the contrary, an engineer of real ability was a necessity aboard, as anyone above the intelligence level of an idiot would know. And it had not been an idiot who had arranged the attack on him in the split seconds of time and space when he would be out of view, just before boarding the shuttle. And unless he were very badly mistaken, there was no one but himself on Lab I capable of the required engineering job; though that situation would probably change with the next shuttle.

Anyhow, he thought, I've probably got the two weeks clear. And, he decided as a second thought, Ishie can probably give me a lot more cogent answers than the Cow can dream up, without nearly the semantic hazard.

He stood and headed for the quarters devoted to the work of Dr. Y Chi Tung.

As he approached the machine shop, next door to the physics lab, the sound of the wailing *Spaceman's Lament* filled the corridor, and he stopped by the open double bulkhead that served as an airlock in emergencies.

Paul Chernov was singing at the top of his lungs while he carefully inspected the alignment of a numeric-controlled laser microbeam milling and boring machine. As

Mike watched, he brought the beam to a focus and pressed an activation switch that started a pattern of tiny capillary holes in the quartz work-piece.

Gently removing the work piece from its mounting, Paul turned toward a side double bulkhead that led into the lab beyond. Mike stepped into the room then, and Paul, seeing him, grinned.

"Whatcha got there?" Mike asked.

"Special milling job for Ishie. Come on. You'll be interested."

Ishie, Tombu at his side, was busy over a haywire rig as the two entered. Glancing up, he bobbed his head at Mike. "Hi," he said, then turned to take the newly-machined part reverently from Paul's hands. "A thousand ancestral blessings," he told the tall, blond youth. "Confusion say the last piece is the most honored for its ability to complete the gadget, and this is it. Of course," he added, "Confusion didn't say whether it would work or not."

"What does the gadget do?" asked Paul.

"Ummm. As the European counterpart of Confusion, Dr. Heisenberg might have explained it, this is a device to confuse confusion by aligning certainties and creating uncertainties in the protons of this innocent block of plastic." The round saffron-hued Chinese face looked at Paul solemnly.

"As the good Dr. Heisenberg stated, there is a principle of uncertainty as to the exact whereabouts of things on the atomic level, which cannot be rendered more exact due to disturbance caused by the investigation of its whereabouts. My humble attempt is to secure a sufficiently statistical sample of aligned protons to obtain data on the distortion of the electron orbits caused by an external electrostatic field, thus rendering my own uncertainties more susceptible of analysis in a statistical manner."

Suddenly he grinned. "It's a take-off," he said, "from the original experiments in magnetic resonance back in '46.

"The fields generated in these coils are strong enough to process all the protons so that their axis of spin is brought into alignment. At this point, the plastic could be thought of as representing a few billion tiny gyroscopes all lined up together.

"Matter of fact," he added in an aside, "if you want a better explanation of that effect, you might look up the maintenance manual on the proton gyroscopes that Sad Cow uses. Or the manuals for the M.R. anaylser in the chem lab. Or the magnetometer we use to keep a check on Earth's magnetic field.

"So far, about the same thing.

"What I'm trying to do is place radio frequency fields and electrostatic fields in conjunction with the D.C. magnetic field, so as to check out the effect of stretching the electron orbits of the hydrogen atoms in predictable patterns.

"I picked this place for it, because it was as far away from Earth's magnetic field as I could get. And Mike, when I get ready to test this thing, I'm going to pray to my ancestors and also ask you to turn off as many magnetic gadgets as you safely can."

Mike was squatting on his heels by the haywire rig, built into what looked suspiciously like a chassis extracted from one of the standard control consoles of the communications department.

Reaching gingerly in through the seemingly confused mass of cables surrounding the central components, he pointed to one of the coils and exclaimed in the tones of a Sherlock Holmes, "Ah-ha, my dear Watson! I have just located the final clue in the Mystery of my Missing Magnaswedge. I suppose you know the duty cycle on those coils is only about 0.01?"

"Not after I finished with them!" Ishie grinned, unrepentant. "Besides, I don't want to squash anything in the field. I just want a nice, steady field of a reasonable magnitude. As Confusion would say, he who squashes small object may unbalance great powers."

While he talked, Ishie had been busy inserting the carefully machined piece of quartz plate that Paul had brought, into a conglomeration of glassware that looked like refugees from the chem lab, and flipped a switch that caused a glowing coil inside a pyrex boiler to heat a small quantity of water, which must escape through the carefully machined capillary holes in the plate he had just installed. Each jet would pass through two grids, and on towards a condenser arrangement from which the water would be recirculated into the boiler by a small pump which was already beginning to churkle to itself.

"O.K.," Mike said. "I dig the magnetic resonance part. And how you're using the stolen coils. But what's this gadget?" and he pointed to the maze of glass and glass tubing.

"Oh. Permit me to introduce Dr. Ishie's adaptation of a French invention of some years previous, which permits the development of high voltages by the application of heat to the evaporation of a fluid medium such as water—of which we have plenty aboard and you won't miss the little that I have requisitioned—causing these molecules to separate and pass at high speed through these various grids, providing electrostatic potentials in their passage which can be added quite fantastically to produce the necessary D.C. field through which. . . ."

As he spoke, Mike's finger moved nearer a knob-headed bolt that seemed to be one of two holding the glass device to its mounting board, and an inch and a half spark spat forth and interrupted the dissertation with a loud "Yipe!"

"Confusion say," Ishie continued as Mike stuck his finger in his mouth, "he who point finger of suspicion should be careful of lurking dragons.

"Anyhow, that's what it does. There are two thousand separate little grids, each fed by its capillary jet, and each grid provides about ninety volts."

Tombu took the opportunity to ask, "Have you got the RF field-phase generator under control yet?" He pointed to still another section of the chassis.

"Oh, yes." The physicist nodded. "See, I have provided a feed-back circuit to coordinate the pick-up signal with the three-phase RF output. The control must be precise. Can't have it skipping around or we don't get a good alignment."

There was a gurgling churkle from the innocent looking maze, as a borrowed aeriator pump from the FARM supplies began returning condensate back to the boiler.

"It's laughing at us," said Paul. "Come on, Tombu. We got work to do."

As the two machinists left, Mike, still hunkered beside Ishie's contraption, looked up at the physicist.

"How'd you happen to know that—well, that I had trouble getting on the shuttle?"

Ishie settled onto his heels beside the big engineer.

"Confusion say it is often well to keep the eyes open when big projects are overhead. I was watching who came on the shuttle, Mike. And everybody came except you. And it seemed to me that it would not be a good idea for you not to be on the shuttle when it took off. Of course we were not supposed to move once we were seated," he added, his voice merry, "but I am a small Chineseman, and people of authority often tend to overlook what just another small Chineseman is doing. And I am also a physicist of a small renown, and people seated around you who are not in authority almost never ask why a physicist even of small renown is doing what he is doing."

He paused a moment, listening to the churkle of the aeriator, then nodded to himself. "So I stood up—not hesitantly, which would have caused questions, and not abruptly which would have brought attention, but as though normally, and I went to the entryport. So I saw that you did have trouble getting to the shuttle, but I also saw that you would get there. So I sat back down."

"One of those men who tackled me was supposed to double for me on the shuttle," Mike said. "I think he would have ridden in the pilot's compartment, and he would have gone to sick bay the minute he got on Lab One. And I think that my assistant, whom I replaced when I came aboard, would have been their chief engineer. My assistant is groundside now, so I figure I've got two weeks before anything more happens."

There was a silence between them for several moments before Ishie said sadly, "No, Mike. No. You have not got two weeks. You have not got two weeks at all. Because the bills come up for voting very soon now, and whatever happens must happen before the bills are voted."

IV

The conversation that Bessie was having with the Cow was something quite other than that which Mike had attempted from his engineering quarters.

While Mike had spoken tentatively, as to a stranger—
or more accurately, like a teenager with his first girl—
Bessie spoke to a cohort. More, it was almost as though
she were in "conversation" with an extension of herself,
as though she instructed her own memory, or arms or
legs.

She envied Mike the vocoder, whose existence she had
just discovered. She envied it, and she would have one
for herself, if she had to resort to blackmail to get it.
Then she corrected herself.

Blackmailing the Blackhawk, she told herself severely,
would not be an apt way to go about the task. Clumsy
and stupid, in fact. It would get his back hairs up, and
you never rouse a tiger. Sweet talk would do the job,
with ease and finesse, and she would get at it as soon as
she got the Cow programmed.

She grinned to herself. Mike had built a whole system
of input and output to the Cow, and nobody, but nobody,
aboard except herself, had the know how to recognize
the fact.

She herself would never have caught on had it not
been for the program she was now writing into the computer; the program for which she had so carefully worked
herself into this position—the program that would lie
dormant unless and until the crisis she expected occurred.

More until than unless, she told herself, and her fingers
danced on the keyboard.

As a first part of that program, the Cow was now
monitoring every action taken aboard, and was storing the
information in a special memory bank, keyed only to her
own command, and filed for reference under the different
areas of the lab. That was memory storage, and a continuing preliminary to any action.

The action part of the program was more complicated,

but she had spent months working it out, and though it would take some hours to write it in, it was not an impossible task.

The key to the program was the recognition of the essential difference between man and computer: the director as versus the directed. Once given a direction and an outline of the signals to which it must react with its vast store of knowledges and its myriad system of interlocks for carrying out reactions, the means to use could be—more or less safely—left up to the logic of reaction which was a computer's functioning.

It would be a computer-to-computer operation.

The average person, she knew, thought of a computer as an isolated entity, capable of functioning only on its own input, capable of reacting only on its own connections.

Even the average computer operator thought in these terms. And if an occasional computer expert recognized the interconnections possible throughout the growing network of automated, memory-bank motivated, programmed equipment that was taking over the drudgery of civilization, it was only the vague recognition accorded in response to a need to extend in a special area the abilities of one unit.

To Bessie, they were all extensions of the Cow—the vast network of computers, from the telephone system through the power generation and distribution webs, including the telesatellites and the TV stations, and down to and including the banking systems of the nations as well as their automated industrial equipment. Even household items that people took for granted in their homes and shops and automobiles and offices, across the planet.

If it was electronically automated, then it would respond to computer input and could be controlled.

Computer to computer. The network of defense command that webbed the planet from the Arctic to the Antarctic—the network that had been, theoretically, destroyed but had been united under Security—and was computerized to the nth degree, and available as a friend in need on computer signal. The network of TV screens that entertained and informed the civilization, was computer controlled, and an ally when properly called upon. Even the planes in the air or the systems by which the materiel for those planes was ordered and delivered and serviced were computer operated, and subject to properly issued commands.

In a very few systems, isolated to the services that they performed, the interdependence of the various automated factors of a civilization had been brought forcibly to the attention of the peoples of that civilization—occasional power blackouts, occasional communications failures. When those things happened, the people recognized for an instant their awesome dependence upon the functioning of the automated technology—then forgot the question as quickly as possible, relegating it to the realm of the specialist, who seldom really understood the vastness of the factors involved.

Computer to computer. The Cow would have the allegiance—or rather, she must not think in human terms —the cooperation of a network that man, its creator, had not even recognized.

That cooperation must be harnessed to the higher goals of man, before it was taken over—in the name of Security—to make man a slave either to itself or to the mentors who planned to captain the system.

Her fingers flew over the keyboard, programming a concept of action, rather than individual actions; outlining a campaign, rather than detail; setting the goals; and keying the concepts of the campaign as reactions to the actions of man.

When the time came, when the program was activated by its key word, the Cow would speak in computereze to the major computers of the planet below—in electronic impulses and patterns that would be unrecorded in the normal output of those computers, and so would never reach the technicians to alert them.

His equipment in its electronic myriads would follow the actions of man as a supple dancer follows a partner, with affirmation of the patterns that led to his individual freedom; but with a subtle balkishness where his steps led to slavery.

Steve Elbertson stood on the magnetic stat-walk of the south polar lock, gazing along the anchor tube to Project HOT ROD five miles away.

There are no experts in the ability to maneuver properly in free-fall, he told himself. Vainly he attempted to quiet his dissatisfaction with his own self-conscious efforts to maintain the military dignity of the United Nations Security Forces in a medium in which a man inevitably lost the stances that to him connotated that dignity.

Awkwardly he attached the ten-pound electric device known to spacemen as the scuttlebug to the flat ribbon cable beneath the anchor tube that would both power and guide him to HOT ROD.

As the wheels of the scuttlebug clipped over the ribbon-cable, one above and two below, and made contact with its two electrically conductive surfaces, the warning light changed to green, and he was cleared to the far end. He swung his legs over the T-bar at the base of the rod which hung down from the drive mechanism, grasped the rod, and pulled the starting lever. A one gee acceleration— maximum of which the bug was capable, gave him quite a jolt, though the pressure settled out quickly to almost zero as he picked up speed and reached the maximum of 20 miles per hour.

Carefully he kept himself from looking 'down' at Earth, riveting his gaze instead on the luminous balloon tethered against blackness, with narrow traceries of anchor tubes extending from its sunward side to a huge focusing mirror. The Project, seen from here, had all the artless qualities of a clown's face with a grotesquely bulbous nose.

HOT ROD. An eight thousand foot diameter balloon; clear plastic on its sunward side to receive the direct solar radiation; silvered on its inner half to reflect that radiation to its central, thirty-five-hundred foot laser cannon; its backside blackened and bathed with liquid nitrogen to cool the rods and dump the excess radiation and heat into the black cold of space.

The laser cannon itself was a telescoping barrel of concentric circles of ruby rods that took the rays reflected to them and transformed their random wavelengths into a single consolidated torrent of coherent power, focused exactly to the reflecting surface of the huge mirror anchor-tubed half a balloon-diameter in front. From the mirror the lashing energy of the coherent beam could be re-focused to any spot on Earth.

For now the ruby rods of the central laser cannon were quiescent, shadowed from the sun by the half-tube trays in which each thirty foot, half-inch tube rested; trays now rotated so that the rods were covered, and the trays reflected back into the balloon the energy directed to this focal line.

The laser rods lay hibernating in pitch darkness; but when the trays were rotated to the inside of the barrel to create a protective shield directly behind each rod, the beam would lash out to the director mirror, and from there . . . to target Earthside, delivering its energy in a 375 megawatt vortex of irresistible might, in a circle expected to be not over twenty-eight feet in diameter.

The project was tethered on a loose cable, so that its sensors could keep it focused on the sun. The cable ran from the control room at the center of the balloon's backside, to the long anchor tube that held it to the big wheel.

HOT ROD had been fully operational for twelve hours now. It would be tested within another two hours, as the slow swing of the satellite complex in its thirty-six hour orbit, lagging the rotation of Earth by only five degrees an hour, brought it over its target—the Greenland ice cap, eighty miles north of Thule Base.

In this test, its needle point, delivering one million watts of energy per square foot if it lived up to expectations, HOT ROD would put a hole a good way through the several thousand feet of glacier in its target area during the fifteen minutes of projected operation; possibly even exposing the bare rock beneath. The rate of energy delivered, whether up to expectations or not, would be many orders of magnitude higher than that delivered by man's largest nuclear weapon measured a few yards from ground zero, and could be a continuous flow of controlled power at the service of mankind.

Today's operation was scheduled primarily as a test of control and aiming, and in energy concentration. Careful coordination by ground control at Security's Thule Base had been made a vital part of that test so that no misalignment, by *accident or intent,* the broadcasts were emphasizing, could possibly bring it to bear on any civilized portion of Earth's surface.

Steve felt a moment of elation. Dr. Pavlov's results and those of Madison Avenue had been learned and learned well, he thought. That HOT ROD was as dangerous as it was powerful was a fact that anyone should realize;

but the *canaille* were so conditioned to having their thinking done for them and handed to them in propaganda releases that it had been easy to ignore this factor as the project got started and while it was being built. It was as easy to condition it into their thinking now, when that factor was necessary to their thinking for Security's purposes.

The peoples of Earth had been happy with "their" power project for the eighteen months required for its construction. But during the past two weeks they had grown uneasy over its power—an uneasiness carefully engendered by radio insinuation and TV implication. They would be ready to heel to their masters when the time came.

For the last two weeks the air waves had been replete with carefully constructed horror plays, many of them built around "mad scientists", some of them resurrected from as long ago as the early '20s. Even Frankenstein and Dr. X had made their returns to the flickering screens that fed the millions the reactions they would exhibit on command. Ultimatums that defied, and ultimatums that resulted in enslaving peoples (to be overcome later by the noble hero with the military bearing) had been the themes on which a majority of the fictions of the screen were based; and the newscasts were suddenly full of references to power plays from the past, from the old days of disunity and insecurity.

Always in the fictions it was the military figure that rescued the threatened, that saved the situation, that was the identifying focus and the hero.

The guilt-theme, the theme of superiority and inferiority, was being played as well—the guilt theme that had been used so effectively by the Chinese communists in the old days to consolidate their millions of subjects into voluntary cooperation; that had been taken over and used to foist off the most fantastic products by the propaganda smiths of Madison Avenue. It was now a major weapon in the arsenal of Security.

If you were man enough, the releases and the fictions and the controlled commercials implied, you were a member of Security. If you were able, you wore the Uniform. If you didn't have quite what it took to win the Uniform, you were still more able than your neighbor if you wore the Security Symbol as a member of one of the many civilian organizations that were "springing" up under carefully fostered conditions across the planet.

Of course, if you couldn't even make the grade to wear that symbol—if you were refused by the Brotherhood even of those lesser organizations—you could safely be disregarded as an unfit, a burden to society, a hanger-on. . . .

It was almost too easy, Steve thought.

The fear-conditioning on Earth had made it possible to rule and enforce the rule on the satellite that the scientists must never be alone in the control booth of HOT ROD, despite the mile-long security records of each. The fear-conditioning on Earth in the last few weeks had put Elbertson and his men in absolute control of the men who controlled the laser.

It also gave him the power, when the time came, to take unquestioned command of the Laboratory; and the rank of general that would formalize that command was already bestowed, ready for activation.

Nails Andersen, Steve reminded himself with amusement, had originated the laser project. He had fought it through against the advice of more cautious souls, and had, through that project, attained command of Space Lab I and its satellite, all in the name of civilian science.

But he had already lost command of the laser project,

and if he didn't recognize that fact it was because his thinking, too, was conditioned to accept that which he was told through the arts of the screen and the controlled newscast. He had had, and had lost, command of the greatest military weapon ever devised, a weapon that he himself had fostered as a power source for the planet that was rapidly eating itself out of its surface sources of power.

The scuttlebug was passing the halfway mark towards the big balloon, and Steve brought his mind back to the work ahead of him. Project HOT ROD was manned twenty-four hours a "day." The new shift of scientists—the ones who would turn on the powerful beam for its test—would come aboard in about half an hour. The men who had put the finishing touches on the project during the past shift would remain another hour. His own crew of Security men shifted at the mid-points of the scientific cadre's tours of duty, so that for the job he had to do here he would be dealing with a continuing crew of his own men.

The job today was that of levering the scientific personnel into a more subservient attitude towards Security. The ruling which put Security in the control room at all times was only two weeks old, and the autocracy with which the military were being shifted from their first position as mere guards into the position of superiors was being applied on a gradient scale.

The scientists had resented the intrusion of Security at first. They had been restless under it. But the military men had held their stance of guardian angels, protective only, until the restlessness subsided. A week ago, Steve had initiated the process of assuming command of the project for the military. It was done subtly—with an order, in place of a request; with an abrogation of prerogatives, among a crew of scientists who scarcely noticed a prerogative when they saw one, but who found themselves taking second place when they noticed. By the assumption of authority over those who seldom gave more than a passing thought to their own positions of authority, or of subordination.

It was subtle and it was effective; and now that the pattern had been established, those same scientists would have to bring themselves to make an open stand if they wished to attempt to win back the positions from which they had been so gently eased. They would have to actively oppose the imposition of the military will that had already been established as conclusive, if they wanted to bring that will into question; and the opportunity for such an open rebellion was never presented.

They deal in the handling of microscopic particles to their will, and do not recognize the forces that bend their own macroscopic selves to the will of their superiors, Steve thought gleefully.

They do not even recognize that we now command the mighty power that they have designed and built for us.

The immensity around him went unheeded as Steve Elbertson, eyes on Project HOT ROD, savored the power of the beam that could control Earth.

In the observatory of Space Lab I, Perk Kimbal and his assistant Jerry were finding the calibration of the many instruments that still remained to be done easier in some ways and more difficult in others in the free fall conditions of the stationary dome free-swinging on the North polar hub of the big wheel. Perk found he retained his gravity-oriented reactions, as Jerry spoke, and he caught himself looking across, rather than angled over his head, for the lanky figure.

"This flare business that our captive Indian was predicting," Jerry was saying. "Think there's anything to it? Am I actually learning about my profession from lay sources?"

"A rather presumptuous prediction, though he may be right." Perk's clipped tone was partly English, partly the hauteur of the professional. To him, solar phenomena were strictly sourced in the sun, and if they were to be understood at all, it would be in reference to the internal dynamics of the sun itself.

Relaxing in mid-air, he turned himself with a light touch on a stanchion so that Jerry was actually across from his gaze, rather than angled above.

"The torroidal magnetic fields dividing the slowly rotating polar regions from the more rapid rotation near the solar equator," he said slowly and rather pedantically, "should have far more effective control over solar phenomena than the periodic unbalance created by the off-center gravitic fields when the inner planets bunch on the same side of their solar orbits.

"To imply otherwise would be rather like saying that the grain of sand is responsible for the tides.

"Yes," he added honestly, "the records compiled by some of the communications interests—they used to be pretty well disturbed by solar flares, y'know—seem to indicate that there is a connection. So there exists the possibility, however remote, that our Chief Engineer might be right—or rather, that there is a force involved that makes the two factors coincidental."

But even as he talked an unnoticed needle on the board began an unusual, wiggling dance, far different from its ordinary, slow, averaging reactions. Twice, without being noticed, it swung rapidly towards the red line on its meter face; and then, on its third approach, the radiation counter swung over the red line and triggered an alarm.

From only one source in their environment could they expect that level of X-ray intensity. Without so much as a pause for thought, as the alarm screamed, Perk reached for the intercom switch and intoned the chant that men had learned was the great emergency cry of space:

"Flare, flare, flare—take cover!"

V

Steve Elbertson, caught between the lab and HOT ROD, resisted the temptation to reverse the scuttlebug and pull himself to a fast stop, as the flare warning from the observatory came to him over the emergency circuit of his suit. It was followed by Bessie's clipped official voice, "A solar flare is in progress. Any personnel outside the ship should get in as rapidly as possible. Personnel in the rim have seven minutes in which to secure their posts and report to the flare-shield area in the hub. Spin deceleration will take effect in three minutes, and we are counting on my mark towards deceleration. Mark, three minutes."

The Security officer squeezed the trigger of the scuttlebug tighter in a vain effort to force it and himself forward at a higher speed.

The lesser shielding of the HOT ROD control room would not provide a sufficient safety factor even for the X-rays that he knew were already around him; but he must supervise the security of the shutdown; and he could only be very thankful that he was already nearly there and would not have to make the entire round trip under these radioactive conditions.

The scuttlebug, tripped by a block signal set in the ribbon cable, began slowing for the end of its run. As it came to a stop at the end of the long anchor tube, Steve dismounted and, one hand on the slack tether cable, kicked over the short remaining distance.

Passing through the air lock to the control room, he reflected that his exposure would probably be sufficient to give him a touch of nausea in the first half hour.

Inside HOT ROD Control, there was little excitement. The equipment was being turned off in the standard approved safety procedures necessary to turn control over to the laser communication beam which would put the project under Earth control at Thule Base, Greenland, until the emergency was over.

This separate, low-power control beam, focused on Thule Base nearly eighty miles away from the main focus of HOT ROD on its initial target, carried all the communications and telemetry necessary for the close coordination between Thule and the project.

As Elbertson entered, the HOT ROD communications officer was switching each of the control panels in turn to Earth control, while Dr. Benjamin Koblensky, project chief, stood directly behind him supervising the process. Elbertson took up his post beside Dr. Koblensky, replacing the Security aide who had had the past shift. "Suit up," he said to the man briefly.

As the communications officer completed the turnover, and the other five scientists in the lab left their posts to suit up, the com officer glanced up, received a nod from Dr. Koblensky, and said into his microphone, "All circuits have now been placed in telemetry security opera-tion. On my mark it will be five seconds to control aban-donment. Mark," he said after another nod from Dr. Koblensky. "Four, three, two, one, release."

His hand on the master switch, he waited for the green light above it to assure him that the communications lag had been overcome, and as the green light came on, pushed the switch and rose from the console.

Major Elbertson stepped behind him, scanned the switches, inserted his key into the Security lock, and turned it with a final snap, forcing a bar home through the handles of all of the switches to prevent their un-authorized operation by anyone until the official Security key should again release them. In the meantime, no func-tions could be initiated within the laser system by anyone other than the Security control officer at Thule Base on Earth.

HOT ROD was secured, and its crew were taking turns at the lock to make the life-saving run back to the flare-shield area in the hub of Lab I.

Last man out, three minutes after the original alarm, Steve glanced carefully around his beloved control booth, entered the now-empty air lock, and reaching the outside dove fast and hard along the slack cable to the anchor tube terminal and the scuttlebug that would take him swiftly to the big wheel and comparative safety.

In the gymnasium that served under emergency con-ditions as the flare-shield area of the hub—long since dub-bed the "morgue"—the circular nets of hammocks that made it possible to pack six hundred personnel into an area with a thirty-two foot diameter and a forty-five foot length, were lowered. They would hardly be packed this time, since less than one-third of the complement were yet aboard.

Even so, each person had his assigned hammock space, two and a half feet wide; two and a half feet below the hammock above; and seven feet long; and each made his way towards his assigned slot.

At one end of the morgue was the area where the cages of animals from the FARM were being stored on flare-shield shelves; and where Dr. Millie Williams was supervising the arrangements of the trays and vats of plants that must be protected as thoroughly as the humans.

At the other end of the morgue, the medics were setting up their emergency treatment area, while nearby the culinary crew pulled out and put in operating condition the emergency feeding equipment.

The big wheel's soft susurrus lullaby had already changed to a muted background roar as her huge pumps drew the shielding waters of the rim into the great tanks that gave the hub twenty-four feet of shielding from the expected storm of protons that would soon be raging in the vacuum outside.

The ship was withdrawing the hydraulic mass from its rim much as a person in shock draws body fluids in from the outer limbs to the central body cavities. The analogy was apt, for until danger passed the lab was knocked out, only its automatic functions proceeding as normal, while its consciousness hovered in interiorized self-protective withdrawal.

On the panel before Bessie the computer's projection of expected events showed the wave-front of protons approaching the orbit of Venus, and on the numerical panel directly below this display the negative count of minutes continued to march before her as the wave-front approached at half the speed of light.

The expected diminishment of X-rays had not yet occurred. Normally, there would be a space of time between their diminishment and the arrival of the first wave of protons, but so far it had not happened.

Six minutes had passed, and the arriving personnel of Project HOT ROD came in through the locks from the loading platform, diving through the central tunnel over Bessie's head and on to the shielded tank beyond.

Seven minutes, then from the Biology lab came an excited voice. "I need some help! I've lost a rabbit. I came back for the one I'd been inoculating, but he got away from me, and I can't corner him in this no-gravity!"

Bessie wasn't sure what to say, but Captain Andersen spoke into his intercom. "Dr. Lavalle," he said in a low voice but with the force ' command, "ninety percent of your shielding has already been withdrawn. Abandon the rabbit and report immediately to the hub."

The pumps were still laboring to bring in the last nine percent of the water that would be brought. The remaining one percent of the normal hydraulic mass of the rim had been diverted to a very small-diameter tube at the extreme inner portion of the rim, and was now being driven through this tube at frantically higher velocities to compensate for the removal of the major mass. In addition, it maintained a small percentage of the original spin, so that the hub would not be totally in free fall, though the pseudo-gravity of centrifugal force had already fallen to a mere shadow of itself, and some of the personnel were feeling the combined squeamishness of the Coriolis effect near the center of the ship and the lessening of the gravity.

As the last tardy technician arrived, the medics were

already selecting out the nearly ten percent of the personnel who had been exposed to abnormally dangerous quantities of radiation during the withdrawal procedure. This group included all of the personnel that had been aboard Project HOT ROD at the time of the flare.

Even as the medics went about injecting carefully controlled dosages of sulph-hydral antiradiation drugs, the beginnings of nausea were evident among those who had been overexposed. However, only the dosimeters could be relied on to determine whether the nausea was from the effects of radiation, the effects of the near-free-fall and coriolis experienced in the hub, or a psychosomatic reaction that had no real basis other than the fear engendered by emergency conditions.

Major Steve Elbertson was already in such violent throes of nausea that his attending medic was having difficulty reading his dosimeter as he made use of the plastic bag attached to his hammock. He was obviously, for the moment at least, one of the least dignified of the persons aboard.

Displays of the various labs in the rim moved restlessly across most of the thirty-six channels of the computer's video panels, as Bessie scanned about, searching for dangerously loose equipment or personnel that might somehow have been left behind.

In the Biology lab, the white rabbit that had escaped was frantically struggling in the near-zero centrifugal field with literally huge bounds, seeking some haven wherein his disturbed senses might feel more at home. It eventually found a place in an overturned wastebasket wedged between a chair and a desk that were both suction-cupped to the floor. Frightened and alone, with only his nose poking out of the burrow beneath the trash of the waste basket, he blinked back at the silent camera through which Bessie observed him, and elicited from her a murmur of pity.

Seven minutes and forty-five seconds. The digital readout at the bottom of Bessie's console showed the computer's prediction of fifteen seconds remaining until the expected flood of protons began to arrive from the sun.

As radiation monitors began to pick up the actual arrival of the wave front, the picture on her console changed to display the real front, only fractionally in advance of the one it had been displaying as a prediction.

The storm of space had broken.

Captain Andersen's voice came across the small area of the bridge that separated them. "Check the rosters, please. Are all personnel secured?"

Bessie glanced at the thirty-two minor display panels, checking visually even as her fingers fed the question to the computer.

The display of the labs, now that the rabbit was settled into place, showed no dangerously loose equipment other than a few minor items of insufficient mass to present a hazard. Next the Cow displayed a final check-out set of figures, indicating that each person was at his assigned, protected station in the morgue, in the engineering quarters, or on the bridge.

"All secure," she told the captain. "Evacuation is complete."

"Well handled," he said to her, then over the intercom: "This is your captain. Our evacuation to the flare-shield area is complete. The ship and personnel are secured for emergency conditions, and were secured well within the time available. I congratulate you.

"The proton storm is now raging outside. You will be confined to your posts in the shield area for somewhere between sixteen and forty-eight hours. When it is possible to predict the time limit more accurately, the information will be given to you."

As he switched out of the ship's annunciator system, Captain Nails Andersen leaned back in his chair and stretched in relief, closing his eyes and running briefly over the details of the evacuation.

Then he realized that it was not just the completed evacuation that was making it possible for him to relax, to give his taut nerves a breathing space.

The test of HOT ROD was inexorably postponed.

Gratefully he let the tensions ease out, tensions that had been building, he noted now in retrospect, for at least two weeks. He could name no pertinent source for them.

Tension, he asked himself, or fear? HOT ROD was completed. Was that the factor that was—well, making his back hair rise? He wasn't a subtle man, and not given to analysing his own reactions—but just why had it seemed to him recently that the testing of HOT ROD held the connotations of a drastic finality rather than of achievement?

The success of HOT ROD was a fulfillment, a goal achieved—surely not an accomplishment to be . . . feared?

In the engineering compartment, Mike was adjusting the power output level down from the full emergency power that had been required to pump the more than five hundred thousand cubic feet of water from the rim to the hub, to a level more in keeping with the moderate requirements of the lab as it waited out the storm.

As he threw the last switch, he became aware of a soft scuffling sound behind him, and turned to see tiny Dr. Y Chi Tung singlehandedly manhandling through the double bulkhead the bulky magnetic resonance device on which he had been working when the flare alarm sounded, and having the utmost difficulty even though the near free-fall conditions made his problem package next to weightless.

The monkeylike form of the erudite physicist, dwarfed by the big chassis, gave the appearance of a small boy trying to hide an outsize treasure. The nonchalant humor with which he characteristically poked constant fun at both his profession and the traditions of his Chinese ancestors, was lacking.

Dr. Ishie was both breathless and worried.

"Mike," he gasped, "I was afraid to leave it unshielded. It might pick up some residual activity. Radiation, that is, from those hydrogen hordes outside." He let the object rest for a moment, mopping his head while he talked.

"Can you hide it in here? I'm not really anxious to have Budget Control know where some of this stuff went— even though I have honorable intentions of returning the components later—and the good Captain down there on the bridge might not consider its shielding important, either, if he knew I'd sabotaged his beautiful evacuation plan to bring my pretty along!" The tone of Ishie's voice indicated his uncertainty as to Mike's reception.

The idea of Dr. Y Chi Tung worrying about any components he might have "requisitioned" seemed almost irreverent to Mike. Budget Control would gladly have offered that eminent physicist a good half of the entire space station, if he had expressed his needs through proper channels—as a matter of fact, anything on board that wasn't actually essential to the lives of those on the satellite.

Ishie, however, seemed genuinely unaware of his true status and the high regard in which he was held. Besides,

Mike suspected him of a constitutional inability to deal through channels.

Recognizing the true sensitivity that underlay Ishie's constant humor and ridicule of himself, Mike kept himself from laughing aloud. The man could have commandeered the assistance of the captain himself in the shielding of whatever he thought it necessary to shield. Instead, he carefully kept his face solemn while he commented: "It ought to fit in that rack over there." He pointed to a group of half-filled racks. "We can slip a fake panel on it. Nobody will be able to tell it from any of the other control circuits."

Ishie heaved a deep sigh of relief, then grinned his normal grin. "Confusion say," he declared, "that ninety-six pound weakling who struggle down shaft with six hundred pound object, even in free fall, should have stood in bed."

It took the two of them the better part of half an hour to get the unit into place, to disguise its presence and to make proper power connections. Ishie had objected at first to connecting it, and Mike explained his insistence, "If it looks like something that works, nobody will look at it twice. But if it looks like something dead, one of my boys is apt to take it apart to see what it's supposed to be doing." He didn't mention his real reason—a heady desire to run a few tests on the instrument himself.

The job done, the two sat back on their heels, admiring their handiwork like bad boys.

"Coffee?" asked Mike.

"Snarl. Honorable ancestor Confusion doesn't even need to tell me what to do now. My toy is safe. I have worked without stopping for two days, and now the flare has stopped me. Confusion decide to relent. He tell me now: 'He who drive self like slave for forty-eight hours is nuts and should be sent to bed.' I hope," he added, "that the hammocks are soft, but I do not think I shall notice. I know just where to go for I checked in once to fool the Secred Cow before I went to get my beautiful. Now I go back again."

And without so much as a thank-you, he staggered out, grasping for handholds to guide himself in a most unspacemanlike manner.

Mike craftily sat back, still on his heels beside the object, and watched until Ishie had disappeared. He then turned his full interest to the playtoy that fortune had placed in his shop.

Without hesitation he removed the false front they had so carefully put in place. He still had a long tour of duty ahead, and it was very unlikely that he would be interrupted, or, if interrupted, that anyone would question the object on which he worked. It would be assumed that it was just another piece of the equipment normally under his care.

Carefully he looked over the circuits, checking in his mind the function of each. Then he went to his stores and began selecting test equipment designed to fit in the empty racks around it. Oscilloscope, signal generator, volt meters and such soon formed a bank around the original piece of equipment, in positions of maximum access.

Gingerly he began applying power to the individual circuits, checking carefully his understanding of each.

The magnetic field effect, Ishie had explained, but this three-phase RF generator—that puzzled him for a while. Then he remembered some theory. Brute strength alone would not cause the protons to tip. Much as a top, spinning off-center on its point, will swing slowly around that point instead of tipping over, the spinning protons in the magnetic field would precess, but would not tip and line up without the application of a rotating secondary magnetic field at radio frequencies, which would make the feat of lining them up easy.

There, then, were two of the components that Ishie had built into his device. A strong magnetic field supplied by the magnaswedge coils—stolen magnaswedge coils if you please—and a rotating RF field supplied by the generator below the chassis. But the third effect? The DC electric field? That one was new to him.

In his mind he pictured the tiny gyroscopes all brought into alignment by the interplay of magnetic forces; and around each proton the tiny, planetary electrons.

Yet it was all very well to think of the proton nucleus of the hydrogen atom as a simple top. Each orbiting electron must also contribute something to the effect.

At that point, Mike remembered, the electron itself would be spinning, a lighter-weight gyroscope, much as Earth has a lighter weight than the sun. The electron, too, had a magnetic field; more powerful than the proton's field because of its higher rate of spin, despite its lighter mass. The electron could also be lined up.

Somewhere in the back of his mind, Mike remembered having read of another effect. The electron's resonance. Electron para-magnetic resonance.

It, too, could be controlled by radio frequencies in a magnetic field—but the frequencies were different, far up in the microwave region; about three centimeters as Mike recalled. He went back to his supply cabinet to get another piece of equipment, a spare klystron that actually belonged to the radar department but that was "stored" in his shop.

At these frequencies, the three centimeter band of the electromagnetic spectrum, energy does not flow on wires as it does in the lower frequency regions. Here plumbing is required. But Mike, among other things, was an expert RF plumber.

Even experts take time to set up klystrons, and it was three hours later before Mike was ready with the additional piece of haywire equipment which carefully piped RF energy into the plastic block.

This refinement by itself had been done before. Some of the others that Mike applied during his investigation probably hadn't—at least not to any such tortured piece of plastic as now existed between the pole faces of the device.

To have produced the complete alignment of both the protons and the electrons within a mass might have been attempted before. To have applied an electrostatic field in addition to this had perhaps been attempted before. To have done all three, at the same time to the same piece of plastic, and then to have added the additional tortures that Mike thought up as he went along, was perhaps a chance combination, repeatable once in a million tries. It was one of those experimental accidents that sometimes provide more insight into the nature of matter than all of the careful research devised by multi-million-dollar-powered teams of classical researchers.

When the contraption was in full operation, he simply sat on his heels and watched, studying out in his mind the circuits and their effects. The interruption of the magnetic resonance by the electrostatic field . . . by the DC . . . with the RF plumbing . . . twisted by . . . each time the concept came towards the surface it sank back as he tried to pull it into consciousness.

Churkling to itself, the device continued applying its alternate fields and warps and strains.

"It's a Confusor out of Confusion by Ishie, who is

probably as great a creator of Confusion as you could ask," Mike told himself, forgetting his own part in the matter. He sat and watched intently, waiting for the concept to come clear in his mind. Presently he went over to his console, found paper and pencils, and began sketching rapidly—drawing the interlocking and repulsing fields, the alignments, mathing out the stresses—in an attempt to visualize just what it *was* that the Confusor would now be doing. . . .

In the Confusor itself, a tiny chunk of plastic, four by four inches square and one-half inch thick, resting in the middle of the machine between the carefully aligned pole-faces of the magnet, was subjected to the cumulatively devised stresses, a weird distortion of its own stresses and of the inertia that was its existence.

Each proton and electron within the plastic felt an urge to be where it wasn't—felt a pseudo-memory, imposed by the outside stresses, of having been traveling at a high velocity towards the north star, on which the machine chanced to be oriented; felt the new inertia of that velocity. . . .

Forty pounds to the square inch, six hundred forty pounds over the surface of the block, the plastic did its best to assume the motion that the warped laws of its existence said that it already had.

It was only one times ten to the minus five of a gravity that the four by half inch piece of carefully machined plastic presented to the sixty-four million pound mass of Space Lab I. But that force was presented almost exactly along the north-south axis of the hub of the ship, and in space a thrust is cumulative and momentum derives per second per second.

The Confusor churkled quietly as the piece of plastic exerted its tiny mass in a six hundred and forty pound attempt to take off toward the north star.

Since the piece itself was rigidly mounted to its frame, and the frame to the ship, the giant bulk of five million cubic feet of water, thirty-two million pounds of mass, plus the matching mass-bulk of the ship itself, responded to the full mosquito-sized strength of the six hundred forty pound thrust. It was moved a fraction of a fraction of a fraction of a centimeter in the first second; a fraction of a fraction in the second; a fraction. . . .

VI

On the bridge, Com Officer Clark had completed transmitting the captain's detailed report of the evacuation to the hub-shield area caused by the solar flare.

On another line, under Bessie's administrations, the computer was feeding the data obtained by the incomplete equipment in the observatory in its automatic operation.

The captain himself was finishing a plastic bottle of coffee, while he wrote up his log.

It was exactly nine minutes since the Confusor had come into full operation.

The fractions of fractions of centimeters had added on the square of the number of seconds; and the sixty-four million pounds of Space Lab I had moved over thirteen meters.

Trailing the wheel ten miles off was the atomic pile, directly attached to its anchor tube, following the ship in its motion. Tightening, each with a whanging snap too tiny to be remarked within the mass of the ship, were the cables that attached the various items of the dump to their anchor finger.

But still free on the loose one hundred meter cable that attached it to its anchor, and which had had fifteen meters of slack when the ship first began its infinitesimal movement, was Project HOT ROD.

Nine minutes and twenty-three seconds. The velocity of the wheel with its increasing mass of trailing items, was five point four six centimeters per second. The four million pound mass of HOT ROD was slowly being left behind.

The cable tautened the final fraction of a centimeter. Its tug was not fast, but was applied very close to the center of gravity of the entire device since most of HOT ROD's weight was concentrated in and around the control room.

Five point four six centimeters per second. Four million pounds of mass.

If the shock had been direct, it would have equaled two point eight million ergs of energy, created by the fractional movement of the mighty mass of the ship against HOT ROD. But the shock was transmitted through the short end of a long lever. The motion at the beam director mirror, a full diameter out from the eight thousand foot balloon that was HOT ROD, was multiplied nearly sixteen thousand times.

HOT ROD rolled on its center of gravity and its beam-director mirror swung in a huge arc. Sixteen thousand centimeters per centimeter of original motion. Eight hundred and seventy three meters in the first second, before the tracking servos took over and began to fight back.

HOT ROD fought at the end of its tether like a mighty jellyfish hooked on the end of a line. Gradually the swings decreased. Four hundred meters; two hundred meters; one hundred meters; fifty meters; twenty-five meters—and it had come back to a nearly stable focus on the sun.

But the beam director had also been displaced, and vibrated. Internally, the communications beam to Thule Base had been interrupted; and the fail-safe had not failed-safely.

The mighty beam lashed out. The vibrations of the directing mirror began placing gigantic spots and sweeps of irresistible energy across the ice cap of Greenland, in an ever-diminishing Lissajous pattern. By the time the servos refocused the communications beam on Thule, there was no Thule; only a burnt-out crater where it had been.

Slowly but surely the giant balloon settled itself to the task of burning a hole through the Greenland ice cap at a spot eighty miles north of the now-burnt-out Thule Base that had been programmed into its servos as a test of its accuracy. It held that focus in spite of the now steady, though infinitesimal, acceleration under which it joined the procession headed by Lab I.

Now that the waves of action and reaction from the shock energy of its sudden start had subsided, HOT ROD was proving very accurate indeed; and its beam focus was proving as small as had been predicted.

But the instruments that would have measured those facts no longer existed.

In the engineering control center of Space Lab I, the Confusor churkled quietly and continued to pit its mosquito might against its now nearly seventy-eight million pound antagonist. The protons and electrons of the plastic that was center to its forces did their inertial best to occupy that position in space towards the north star in which the warped fields around them forced them to belong.

The mosquito strained its six hundred and forty pound thrust against its giant in the per second per second acceleration that was effective only in the fraction of a fraction of a fraction of a centimeter in the first second, but that compounded its fractions per second. . . .

On the quiet bridge, the captain looked up as Com Officer Clark said, "Thule Base, sir," and switched on his mike.

"HOT ROD has been sabotaged," a frantic voice on the other end of the beam shouted in his ear without formality. "She's running wild! Kill her! Repeat. HOT ROD is wild. Kill HOT ROD. Kill. . . ." the mike went dead even as Captain Andersen switched on the morgue intercom.

"HOT ROD crew," he said briefly. "Report to the bridge on the double. Repeat. HOT ROD crew. The bridge. On the double."

As he switched off the intercom, Communications Officer Clark spoke urgently. "Captain. I've lost contact with Thule Base."

"Keep trying to raise them," the captain said. He turned to Bessie. "Give me a display of the Hellmaker." Then he added, almost to himself, "There's still a flare in progress out there. We've got to kill it without sending men into that. . . ."

He cut himself off in midsentence as the computer displayed both HOT ROD, swaying gently as she fought the battle of the focus through its final moments, and a telescopic view of Greenland, a tiny, glowing coal of red showing at the center of the focus.

Through the bulkhead nearly catapulted the first of the Project HOT ROD crew, followed almost on his heels by twelve more.

"Where is Major Elbertson?"

"In sick bay, sir. He got a big radiation dose. . . ."

The captain flipped the intercom key.

"Calling Major Elbertson in sick bay. Report to the bridge on the double, no matter what your condition. This is the captain speaking."

The intercom came alive at the far end.

"This is Dr. Green, Captain Andersen. Major Elbertson is unconscious. He cannot report for duty. He was extremely ill from exposure to radiation and we have administered sulph-hydral, anti-spasmodic, and sedative."

Nails Andersen turned to the probject crew.

"Which of you are Security officers?"

Three men stepped forward.

"Are all the project members here?"

"No, sir," said one. "Eight of our men are in sick bay."

"Very well," said the captain. "Now hear this, all of you. There is a saboteur—maybe more than one, we do not know—among you. There is no time to find out which of you it is. However, he has managed to leave Project HOT ROD operational while unattended. You are to turn it off and to prevent the saboteur from stopping you. Do you understand?"

A voice in back—a rather high voice—spoke up. "Of course it's operational," it said. "We left it operational."

"You . . . *what?*"

"We left it operational. It's under Earth control. The control center at Thule is in charge, sir."

"Who are you?" the captain asked.

"HOT ROD communications officer, sir. I turned it over last thing before we shut down. Under the instructions of Dr. Koblensky. That's the shutdown procedure during test."

"Where's Dr. Koblensky?"

"Out. Out like a light . . . sir," said another voice. "He got a good dose. Of radiation. The medics put him out."

"Who's senior officer here?"

"I'm Dr. Johnston." It was a man in front. Rather small. Pedantic looking. "I'm Dr. Koblensky's . . . well, assistant." The word came hard as though the fact of an assistantship were at the least distasteful.

"Who's senior in Security?"

"I, sir. Chauvenseer."

"Very well. Dr. Johnston and Chauvenseer are in charge. Now shut down that ruby hellmaker as fast as it can be done."

"But, Captain," Dr. Johnston spoke, "we can't turn it off. We haven't the authority. We haven't the Security key. And the radiation won't let up for hours."

"I have just given you the authority. As for the radiation, that is a hazard you will have to take. What's this about a Security key?" The captain's voice was not gentle.

"Major Elbertson has the key. He has the only key. Without it, the station cannot be removed from Earth control. Earth *is* in control. They can turn it off, Captain." Dr. Johnston's voice took on as firm a tone of authority as that of the captain.

"Chauvenseer!" barked the captain. "Get that key!" He waited until the Security officer had disappeared through the bulkhead, then turned to the scientist.

"Dr. Johnston, Earth is not in control. I do not know why, and there is no way of finding out. HOT ROD is wild, and *that,*" he pointed at the enlarging red spot that centered the computer display, "is what our ruby is doing to Earth.

"You will turn off the project, at gunpoint if necessary," he continued in a grim voice. "If you turn it off volitionally, you will be treated for radiation. If you refuse, you will not live to be treated for anything. Do you understand? How many men do you need to help you—and I do mean *you*—with the job?" he asked.

Dr. Johnston hesitated only fractionally, and Nails Andersen mentally put him down on the plus side of the personnel, for the shortness of his comlag. Then he said crisply, "The job will require only two men for the fastest accomplishment. You realize, Captain, that you are probably signing our death warrants—the two of us. But," he added, glancing only casually at the display on the console, "I can understand the need to sign that warrant, and I shall not quibble."

The intercom spoke. "This is Dr. Green, Captain. There is no key on the person of Major Elbertson. We have searched thoroughly, sir. I understand the need is of an emergency nature. The key is not on his person. We have taken every possible measure to arouse him, as well, and have not been successful."

Andersen flipped his switch. "Let me speak to the Security officer I sent in," he said briefly.

"Chauvenseer speaking, sir," the man's voice came on.

"Do you know what the key looks like?"

"Yes, sir. It looks somewhat like a common Yale key, sir. But I've never seen another just like it."

"There is only the one?"

"Yes, sir."

"Where would he keep it, if not on his person?"

"I don't know, sir. We came straight to the morgue—the shield area, from the air lock. I don't believe he stopped off anywhere he could have put it."

The captain turned to the second Security officer.

"Search Elbertson's space suit," he said. Then to the intercom, "Search his hammock. Search every spot he went near. That key must be found in minutes. Comandeer as many men as can help in the search without getting in the way."

He paused a moment, then flipped another intercom key.

"Mr. Blackhawk," he said.

The intercom warmed at the far end. "Yes sir?" Mike's voice was relaxed.

"Is there any way to turn off HOT ROD without the Security key?"

"Why sure, Captain," Mike's voice held a grin. "I could pull the power switch."

"Pull it. Fast. HOT ROD's out of control."

Mike's hand flashed to a master switch controlling the power that fed HOT ROD, blessing as he pulled the switch the fallacy of engineering that had required external power to power the mighty energy collector.

In the big balloon, now happily following the wheel at the end of its tether, the still-undamaged power-off failsafe went into operation. The half-tube tray behind each ruby rod rotated into its shielding position, dispersing back into space the energy that the huge, silvered, bowl-like half of its interior directed towards the rods.

HOT ROD was secure.

Mike received only one further communication from the captain.

"Mr. Blackhawk," he was asked over the intercom, "is there any way that you can secure that HOT ROD power switch so that it cannot be turned on without my personal authorization?"

"Sure, Captain, I can. . . ."

The captain interrupted. "Mr. Blackhawk. I should

prefer that you not tell me or anyone else aboard the method you will use, and that you make your method as difficult as possible to discover. This I shall leave," he added dryly, "to your rather . . . fertile . . . imagination.

"There is reason to believe that Project HOT ROD was turned on by a saboteur. Your method must be proof against him, and if he exists, he will not be stupid." The captain switched off.

Mike turned to the control panel, and after a few minutes' thought busied himself for some time.

Then he headed for the bridge where Dr. Johnston, Chauvenseer, and the captain had dismissed the others and were utilizing every check that Dr. Johnston could devise to assure themselves that HOT ROD was actually turned off and would remain secure at least for the duration of the flare; and trying as well to find out just what form the sabotage had taken.

At the communications console, Clark murmured busily to Earth.

Without interrupting the others, Mike seated himself at the subsidary post on Bessie's right at the computer console, and got her to brief him. He listened while he examined the close-up display of HOT ROD, searching for any clue to the method used, as the others were doing.

Then, abruptly, he reached over and increased the magnification to its maximum, until the picture showed only a small portion of the balloon; then moved the focus to display the air lock to the control room as well as part of the anchor tube and the cable between.

In the face of danger, he thought, *it is very easy to attribute to the enemy anything—coincidental or accidental—that may happen. It is easy,* he thought, *and a very great mistake.*

Nevertheless, he checked over carefully the possibility of human agency in the particular form of "sabotage" he was beginning to suspect, discarding the possibility before turning to the others.

"I think I've found your saboteur," he said, grimacing wryly.

The captain was at his side almost instantly. "Where is he?" he asked, his voice tense.

"Not he, sir. It. And I'm not sure just where—but look. HOT ROD's cable is taut. That means there's thrust on the balloon. That probably means a puncture and ex-caping nitrogen.

"I think," he added slowly, "that the saboteur may have been a meteor that punctured the balloon, and the nitrogen escaping is creating a jet action, producing enough thrust to keep the cable taut. Though," he added, "I don't see why the servos couldn't maintain the beam to Thule—even though, obviously, they didn't."

"How sure are you that a human saboteur could not have made such a puncture?"

"Not 'could not,' Captain, but 'would not.' A saboteur would have wanted to accomplish something if he were going to take a chance like that aboard a small base like this. He'd have to want to accomplish something very exact. Now a puncture in the balloon *might* do something —it *did* do something very drastic—but the chances were just as good that there would be no result at all, aside from a small mending job and extra work for the nitrogen pumps. It's a real outside possibility that a puncture only big enough to cause a small jet effect would throw off the control beam and turn on the laser. So it's not something a saboteur would do. If he wanted to hurt the project, there were a dozen better possibilities open to him. And there's no way there could be thrust on that balloon that

I can think of, other than from a small puncture-jet."

"How dangerous is such a puncture?" asked the captain. "How seriously would HOT ROD be damaged? How soon must it be repaired?"

"The puncture itself shouldn't be too dangerous. The servos are still keeping the balloon properly oriented; and even if all the nitrogen except that in the servos goes the balloon's in a vacuum and won't collapse; and that's the only other serious effect a puncture would have. Just a moment. We'll estimate the size of the puncture by the amount of thrust it's giving the ship."

He turned to Bessie. "Ask the Cow whether we're getting thrust on the ship; and if so, how much. Wait a minute," he added. "If you ask for thrust on the ship, she'll say there isn't any, because HOT ROD would be pulling us, not pushing. And if you ask her for the thrust on HOT ROD, she hasn't got any sensors out there.

"Hmmm. Ask her if we have added any off-orbit velocity, and if so how much."

The computer displayed the answer almost as soon as she received the question.

"Well," said Mike, "that's not too large a hole. Ask her how . . . let's see . . . how many pounds of thrust that velocity represents. That way we don't confuse her with whether it's push or pull."

The Cow displayed the answer, *six hundred and forty pounds of thrust.*

"Okay," said Mike. "Thanks." Then to the captain, the scientist and the Security officer who were waiting beside him: "The puncture is obviously small enough to serve as a jet, rather than to have let the nitrogen out in one *whoosh,* since that would have given you far more than six hundred forty pounds of thrust. Therefore, it will probably be quite simple to patch the hole.

"Nitrogen is obviously escaping, but it wouldn't be worth a man's life to send him out into that flare-storm to patch it, now that the Hellmaker's shut down and can't do any more damage under any circumstances. We may even have enough nitrogen aboard to replace what we lose.

"The best I can figure," he said, "is that the meteor must have hit the orientation servos after it got into the balloon, and thrown them off for a bit; but they're obviously all right now, because they're oriented. We'll have to wait until after the flare to make more than an educated guess, though, as to exactly what happened.

"We shouldn't be too far off-orbit by the time the flare's over, either, even if that jet stays constant. It'll take quite a bit of work, but we should be able to get back on orbit with not too many hours of lost work time.

"Except for Thule, I'd say we got off fairly light.

"Yes," he added grimly, "it looks like that's what your saboteur was. Rather an effective saboteur, but you'll have a hard time putting him up before a firing squad."

Having satisfied himself as to existing conditions, Mike excused himself shortly and went back to the engineering quarters, but his mind was no longer on Ishie's strange device. He glanced rapidly over the readings on the instruments regulating the power flow to the wheel, then stretched out comfortably on the acceleration couch and in minutes was asleep.

The Captain, Dr. Johnston and Chauvenseer remained on the bridge for another hour, convincing themselves that Mike's analysis was correct, and dictating a report to Earth, before the captain called in an aide to take over the bridge, and the three retired.

Bessie gave over the Cow to one of her assistants, and left to get coffee, some conversation, and some sleep.

In the morgue, Dr. Y Chi Tung, who still slept peacefully as he had since the moment he reached his hammock, muttered quietly in his sleep, "Confusion. . . ."

Chad Clark placed a small mirror on the communications console before him in such a way that he could watch the quiet figures at the Captain's and the Cow's consoles. The youngster who served as the captain's aide was writing busily; the young man who monitored the Cow was reading.

Using the hush-mike that made it possible for him to keep a constant flow of communication to Earth without disturbing others on the bridge, Clark started to activate the private Security channel hidden on his board, then held his hand until the now-soporific atmosphere on the bridge could take greater effect on the others.

Was it an accident? The question had raged through his consciousness from the moment that Thule Base had come through with its desperate plea, and it had taken the utmost in self-control to keep him from using the private channel to query those who would know. Accident or not, his job was to maintain the front of a normal communications chief, until instructions from the C.O. or from Earth bade him do otherwise—or until operation Ripe Peach was officially under way.

But—if it were intentional—why Thule Base? Why a Security stronghold? Such a ruse would have obvious advantages in pointing guilt away from Security—but *our own men?*

He couldn't doubt that Thule was gone. That fact was clear, both from the glowing coal that had brillianted on the Cow's screens, and from the sincerely horrified voices that had constantly through the channels from Earth, demanding explanations, asking searching questions, making suggestions. He'd passed on a few of those suggestions to the captain who, after the Hellmaker was finally turned off, had asked him to screen communications for only the most important so that he could keep his attention on the problem.

But . . . it would be so improbable that an accident could have nearly duplicated the exacting plans of Ripe Peach. Yet, if it were purposeful, why had he not been alerted? Why a time when the C. O. was laid out flat, knocked out, in sick bay? Why . . . *now*? The timing was all wrong unless—chills ran down his back—unless the entire Security crew aboard had been labelled "expendable."

He could wait no longer. He keyed the private channel, and was answered almost immediately.

"Clark. Lab I," he said briefly. The repeats and as many as possible of the formalities were dispensed with on this channel, where privacy of communication was essential. This was not a scrambled hookup. Rather, his words would go through as a code pattern of telemetry signals mixed into the other millions of bits of data that were constantly flowing through the beams to Earth on a pre-selected "random" basis which was designed to be ignored by all but the special receiver built for the purpose of picking it up.

His voice would arrive in the clear, but in transit would be mixed with the telemetry signals in an unintelligible pattern that would be discarded by the ordinary telemetry receiver. The security estimate for this type of transmission was one part in ten to the ninth—a very high order of security. Even so, communications were kept as short as possible, limiting even further the possibility of accidental pickup.

"Was it an accident?" Clark asked.

"That's what I've been waiting to ask you," the voice at the other end snapped after the brief communications lag.

"It seems, from this end, to have been an accident." Clark's clipped voice covered his confusion. "The formal reports you have been receiving over regular channels are accurate so far as I can ascertain from this post."

The lag that followed was longer than just a communications lag caused by the distance involved. Then: "I will have your orders shortly. Take no overt action until they are received." The channel blanked.

A few minutes later the private channel signalled through again.

"How is radio reception up there during this flare?" Clark was asked.

"Nil," he answered. "Communication is currently confined to the beams and must go through this board."

"Fine," said the other voice, almost laconically, and blanked the channel again.

On Earth, a hastily called conference of four in the top echelon of Security headquarters was only one of many actions being carried out.

All over the world, Security Headquarters were being alerted to a standby basis; cadres of men were being called out; preparedness procedures were being put into operation. But the alert was only yellow.

It had hardly been necessary to call an alert. The news of the catastrophe at Thule Base was on every TV screen across the world. Officials of every nation were gathering without being summoned. Lights in U.N. Headquarters were switching on as rapidly as the representatives of the nations received the news and reached their offices. It would be merely a gesture to call an Assembly; those who would be assembled were ready and waiting.

No explanations had yet been forthcoming. The planet waited, fearfully.

No news had been forthcoming, because in the conference room at Security Headquarters the decision had not been made as to just what purport the follow up on the fact of the catastrophe was to be allowed to have.

A speaker on the center of the table around which the four sat was carrying both sides of the conversation with Clark on the satellite. As the speaker blanked, the highest-ranking of the four reached forward and switched it off.

"I think we can safely assume," he said, "that Thule was an accident. Certainly Andersen would have tracked down any other possibility by now. Or, if it had been another group with our own intentions, they would have shown their hand by now.

"However, to allow Thule to remain an accident would leave a question in people's minds, when our own operations are initiated, that these, too, might be based on accidental circumstances. This question must not be permitted. Our plans are similar to this accident—they will not falter for being shifted to this circumstance. Details of the timing can be worked out."

There was no argument—only a short discussion of detail.

Operation Ripe Peach was go.

Mike snapped awake and glanced guiltily at the clock. Six hours had passed.

A situation report from the Cow was the first thing on his agenda any time that he had been out of contact for any length of time, flare or not. Now it was especially important.

He couldn't, though, simply ask for a situation report. If he did that, he'd have received such miles of data that he'd be listening for hours. Instead, as he keyed the voco-der, he broke his questions down into the facets that he needed.

In a few minutes he had elicited the information that solar flare conditions were predicted to ameliorate within ten hours, at which time the major part of the flare protons would be past the laboratory orbital position. Earth coordi-nates had shifted, indicating the lab orbital shift to have been a trifle over thirty-seven kilometers north in the past eight hours. . . .

North? he thought. *HOT ROD's pull on a taut cable would be to the south.*

No. Lab I could be reoriented to trail the thrusting balloon. But the lab's servos should have prevented that reorientation unless the thrust were really heavy.

"What is our velocity?" he asked. Temporarily he was baffled by the placid Cow's literal translation of his request as one for an actual velocity, since it replied with a figure very close to their original orbital speed.

"What is our velocity at right angles to our original course?" he asked.

And the Cow's reply came: "Two hundred and fifty-seven point seven six centimeters per second."

That should be about right for six hundred forty pounds of thrust for, say, six and a half hours; and the distance of the orbit shift was about right.

But the direction?

"Is HOT ROD pulling us north?" he asked.

"No," came the placid reply.

"If it's pulling us south, then why. . . ." He stopped

himself. Any "why" required inductive reasoning, and of that the Cow was not capable. Instead of asking why they were moving north with a south thrust, Mike broke his question into parts. He'd have to answer the "why" himself, he knew.

"Is HOT ROD pulling us south?" he asked.

"No," came the answer.

This time he was more careful. "In which direction is the thrust on HOT ROD oriented?" he asked.

"North."

"Then HOT ROD is. . . ." Quickly he stopped and rephrased the statement which would have had a question in its tone but not in its semantics. He changed it to a question that would read semantically. "Is HOT ROD pulling us north?"

"No," came the reply.

Carefully. "Is HOT ROD pulling us?"

"No."

Mike was stumped. Then he figured a literalness in his phrasing.

"Is HOT ROD pushing or in any other way giving motion to Space Lab I?" he asked.

"No," came the answer.

Now Mike *was* stumped.

"Is Space Lab I under acceleration?" he asked.

"Yes," said the Cow.

"Then where in hell is that acceleration coming from?" Mike was exasperated.

"We are under no acceleration from hell," the literal mind told him.

Mike laughed ruefully. No acceleration from hell—well, that was debatable. But no thrust from the Hellmaker was not a debatable point. The Cow wasn't likely to be wrong, though her appalling literalness was such that an improperly phrased question might make her seem to be.

Computers, he thought, would eventually be the salvation of the human race, whetting their inventors' brains to higher and higher efforts towards the understanding of communications.

Very carefully now he rephrased his question. "From what, and from what point, is the acceleration of Space Lab I originating?"

"From the continuous thrust originating at a point thirteen feet from the axial center of the wheel, in hub section five north, one hundred twelve degrees from reference zero of the engineering longitude reference station assigned in the construction manual dealing with relative positions of mass located on Space Lab I."

Mike glanced up at the tube overhead, which represented the axial passageway down the hub of the wheel. Thirteen feet from the imaginary center of that tube, and in his own engineering compartment.

Then his gaze travelled on around the oddly built, circular room with its thirty-two foot diameter. The reference to hub section five north meant this compartment. The degrees reference referred to the balancing coordinates by which the Cow kept the big wheel statically balanced during rotation. There was a bright stripe of red paint across the floor which indicated zero degrees; and degrees were counted counterclockwise from the north pole of the wheel.

His eyes strayed across the various panels and racks and came to rest in the one hundred twelve degree area. A number of vacant racks, some holding the testing equipment he had moved there not too many hours before . . . and, churkling quietly in its rack near the floor, Ishie's Confusor of Confusion.

Mike contemplated the device with awed respect, then phrased another question for the Cow.

"Exactly how much thrust is being exerted on that point?" he asked.

The computer reeled off a string of numbers so fast that he missed them, and was still going into the far decimal places when Mike said: "Whoa! Approximate number of pounds, please."

"Approximately six hundred and forty. You asked for exact figures, and did not specify any limits of accuracy." The burred tone was still complacent.

"Just what acceleration has that given us?" asked Mike, still looking at the Confusor. "Approximately," he added quickly.

"Present acceleration is approximately eight point nine five times ten to the minus third centimeters per second per second. I can carry that to several more decimal places if you wish."

"No thanks. I think you've told me enough. For now," he remembered to add.

Mike stood up.

This, he thought, needs Ishie . . . and coffee.

Then he turned back to his secret vocoder panel and said: "The information you have just given me is to be regarded as top secret and not to be discussed except over this channel and by my direct order. Absolutely nothing that would give any one a clue to the fact that there is a method of acceleration aboard. Understood?"

"Yes."

"Okay."

Mike switched off the vocoder, flipped his intercom to the temporary galley in the morgue, and ordered two breakfasts readied. Then he set off.

VII

Chad Clark didn't dare leave the communications console, and he didn't dare let anyone know he was refusing to leave.

The man who was scheduled to relieve him was easily handled. Clark simply messaged him that shift schedules had been revised and that he would be alerted when his duty time on the new roster came up.

But the other members of the Bridge personnel?

No one had seemed to notice. They've assumed that I arrived for duty just before they did, he decided. Perhaps I could use the same ruse when Bessie and the captain return. . . .

No messages at all were coming through the board. That was unusual, even for normal operation; and after such a catastrophe as had just occurred it was quite impossible that messages should not be pouring towards the satellite from all over Earth. But the board was silent.

They've blanked us, he thought. So something *is* happening, or rather something is being made to happen. He tried to listen through the static of the radio, but the screeching electronic violence of the space-storm outside made it impossible to pick up any part of any Earth broadcast.

The long hours wore on, and Clark found himself nodding before the console. Hastily he pulled himself awake, slipped stim-pills from his pocket and gulped them.

Five hours had passed before the private channel came alive at last. Plugging a switch into the main board so that it would appear that he was talking over normal channels, he switched it on.

"LeClare, Earth," the voice said. "Clark?"

"Chad Clark, sir."

"Are you receiving radio broadcasts up there yet?"

"No, sir. No radio, no communication on the board, no communication at all."

"What is the situation up there?"

"Everyone is convinced that the Thule thing was an accident, sir, caused by a meteor on the big balloon. The captain and the systems control officer have retired; their aides are on duty. I believe the chief engineer is asleep, but his quarters are not in view here."

"How long have you been on duty, Clark?"

"Since about four hours before the flare, sir. Only about thirteen hours."

"How are you holding up? Can you handle things awhile longer?"

"As long as necessary, sir. I'm fine, sir."

"All right. We're depending on that. Don't leave that board. Now. Is Major Elbertson alerted to the situation yet?"

"Major Elbertson is still unconscious, sir."

"Hmmm. Not good. Do you have any idea whether he could be brought out of it in fairly good condition yet?"

"I don't know, sir, but right after . . . Thule, the medics tried to bring him out, but the sedation was too heavy and they couldn't rouse him at all."

"Well. So long as nobody on board has any idea what's going on, we can operate without him. If he were brought out now, he might be groggy. We'll wait until it becomes absolutely necessary, then send orders for the medics to bring him out if he's not already out by then. You sure you're the only one aboard who knows what's going on?"

"Yes, sir. Except that I don't know what's going on, sir."

The voice laughed. "That radio blank-out must be

pretty thorough. But nobody else suspects that anything's going on?"

"No, sir—but sir, the captain, when he comes back, will expect messages from Earth, and will be suspicious if there aren't any."

"Good boy, Clark. You're right. Hmmm. Well, there are a few things that we need to know from up there, and I guess we could send the sort of messages that would get us the information. For one thing, it wasn't a meteor that caused whatever happened. I've had the tracking stations checking for all they're worth and you're too far off orbit for that kind of action. So there's the definite possibility that some other organized force aboard is trying to do what we were planning to fake. Clark, is there any possibility that it is the captain who caused Thule to be burned? Think carefully, Clark. Is there any *possibility*?"

Clark thought over the scenes on the bridge from the moment of the call from Thule. The captain's reactions had seemed real, but . . . a competent actor could have handled the role, might have handled it in just that way. And the captain had waited for Blackhawk to remember the power switch. . . .

"It's possible, sir. I'd doubt it, but it's possible."

"What about Blackhawk?"

"I guess . . . I guess that's possible too, sir."

"Hmmmm. Well, we won't assume it is, because it might not be; but we won't assume it isn't, either. I think I'll relay some of the messages that have come in and that the senders think have been relayed to you. We'll have to reword them, though. Especially the ones intimating that we on Earth know that it wasn't a meteor, and that we suspect sabotage or possibly a major attack on Earth. That would be about what he'd expect, if he's the guy; and if he's not, he'll be helping us look for who is.

"Okay, Clark. Your orders are to stay on that board. Don't let anybody else get in communication with Earth. Send on through whatever you're given to send through, because we've got all your lines covered, but let us know the minute that radio reception up there clears and you guys can hear what's going on, because by the time they can listen in, we've got to be already in action up there."

"Yes, sir. Shall I blank the normal data lines to Earth —the ones that are relaying the data from the observatory and from the ship's servos? Those don't go through this board, and I'd have to get assistance——"

"Hmmm. No. Keep those going. Might appear abnormal if you shut them off. Somebody might notice. Now, stand by to receive messages. The time-note on each message will be used as the time you received the message up there. Right?"

"Right, sir. But the captain's still asleep, and—if I might suggest?—if any of those messages seem to require it, I'd have to have him waked. And it's going to be a lot easier to keep him from getting suspicious while he's asleep than when he's on the bridge."

"Very cogent, Clark. Very cogent indeed. Very well. The messages will be innocuous until we hear from you that the captain is on the bridge. Then we'll start sending some dillies. Alert us at once when he comes on. Then we'll keep him so busy he can't get in your hair. Your file will reflect your work this day, Clark. Rest assured that you will be very proud of that file."

As the line blanked, Clark studied the figures at the other consoles, reflected in his tiny mirror. Neither appeared to have noticed the long conversation. Each was busy, probably at make-work, he decided.

It was another fifteen minutes before the "messages" began to dribble through. He relaxed as he assured himself that not one of them was such as would require that he wake anyone in authority.

Mike located Ishie's hammock and nudged the scientist unceremoniously. The small physicist awoke and attempted to sit up in one gesture; bumped his head against the hammock above, and lay back down just as suddenly.

"Come on down to engineering, will you, Ishie?" The request was spoken softly.

"Hokey, dokey," Ishie whispered back and crawled out of the narrow aperture with the agility of a monkey.

Gesturing to the other to follow him, Mike led the way to the galley first, where the two picked up the readied breakfasts, then took them to Mike's quarters.

The "cups" of coffee were squeeze bottles; the trays were soft plastic packages similar to the boil-in-the-bag containers of frozen food that had been common on Earth for some time.

Mike hesitated at the entrance to his engineering quarters, considering whether to shut the bulkhead, but discarded the idea as being more of an attention-getter than a seal for secrecy. He gestured Ishie to the bunk, and parked himself at his console.

"We're in trouble," he said. "You and I together are responsible for the first space attack on Earth."

He stopped and waited, owl-eyed, but the small physicist simply tackled his breakfast with no further comment than a raised eyebrow.

"We," said Mike solemnly, "wiped out Thule Base last night."

"As Confusion would say, there's no Thule like a dead Thule. What are you getting at, Mike? You sound serious."

"You mean you slept through . . . you didn't know we . . . you didn't hear the . . . yes, I guess you slept! Well. . . ."

Rapidly Mike sketched the events of the past nine hours, bringing the story completely up to date, including the information he'd gleaned from the Cow, but making no reference to his access to the computer's knowledge. Instead, he attributed the conclusions to himself.

The physicist sat so still when he had finished that Mike became seriously concerned. "Thule. . . ." he began, but Ishie started to speak.

"Mike, it did? It couldn't . . . but . . . of course, it must have . . . the fields . . . six hundred forty pounds of thrust! Only six hundred forty, yet . . . yes, it could, if the thrust were exactly aligned . . . thrust. Mike, thrust! Real *thrust*! Mike, do you know what this means?" His eyes were alight. His voice was reverent. He sprang from the bunk and knelt before the rack that held the churkling Confusor.

"My pretty," he said. "My delicate pretty. What you have done! Mike, we've got a space drive!"

"Ishie. Don't you realize? *We* wiped out Thule!"

"Thule, schmule—Mike, we've got a space drive!"

Mike grinned to himself. He needn't have worried. Not about Ishie, anyhow.

But now Ishie was gesturing him over.

"Mike," he said, "you must show me in detail. In exact detail. What did you do? What was your procedure?"

Mike came over and casually reached towards the churkling device, saying, "Why, I. . . ." but Ishie reacted with catlike swiftness, blocking the man before he could even touch the rack.

"No, don't touch it. Just *tell* me what you did."

Carefully, now, Mike began outlining in detail his inspection of the device and each step he had taken as he added to its complexities.

When he had finished, the two sat back on their heels thinking. Finally, Mike spoke.

"Ishie, will you please tell me just how does this thing . . . this Confusor . . . *get* that thrust? Just exactly what is involved here?"

Ishie took his time answering, and when he did his words came slowly. "Ah, yes. Confusor it is. I was attempting to confound Heisenberg's statement, but instead I think that between us we have confused the issue.

"Heisenberg said that there is no certainty in our measurement of the exact orbit of an electron. That the instrument used to measure the position of the electron must inevitably move the electron. The greater the attempt at precise measurements, the greater the error produced by the measurements.

"It was my hope," he went on, "to provide greater accuracy of measurement by the use of statistics over the vast number of electrons in orbit around the hydrogen atoms within the test mass. But this, apparently, will not be.

"Now to see what it is that we have done.

"First, let us make a re-expression of the laws of math-physics. You understand that I am feeling my way here, for what we have done and what I thought I was doing are quite different, and I am looking now with hindsight at math-physics from the point of the reality of this thrust.

"As I understand it, there is a mutual exclusiveness of particles, generally expressed by the statement that two particles may not occupy the same space at the same time.

"But as I would put it, this means that each particle owns its own place. Now, inertia says that each particle not only owns its own place, but owns its own temporal memory of where it's going to be unless something interferes with it.

"Now let me not confuse you with semantics. When I say 'memory' and 'knowing' I am not implying a sentient condition. I am speaking of the type of memory and knowing that is a strain in the structure of the proton or atom. This is . . . well, anyhow, not sentient. You will have to translate for yourself.

"So to continue, inertia, the way I would put it, says that each particle not only owns its own place, but owns its own temporal memory of where it is going unless it is interfered with. In other words, the particle arriving here, now, got here by remembering in this other sense that it was going from there to there to there with some inherent sort of memory. This memory cannot be classified as being in relation to anything but the particle itself. No matter how you move the things around it, as long as the things around it don't exert an influence on the particle, the particle's memory of where it has been and where it's going form a continuous straight line through space and must, therefore, have coordinates against which to form a 'memory' pattern of former and future action.

"Now as I understand gravity, it is simply the statement that all the particles of space are covetous, in this same non-sentient sense, of the position in space of all their neighboring particles. In other words, it's a contravention or the attempted contravention of the statement that two particles may not be in the same place at the same time. It seems that all particles have an urge to try to be in each other's space. And this desire is modified by the distance that separates them.

"This adds up to three rules:

"1. No two particles may occupy the same space at the same time.

"2. Even though they can't, they try.

"3. They all know where they're going, and where they've been without relation to anything but the spatial coordinates around them.

"That third statement would knock some holes in Einstein's theory of relativity, *unless you wish to grant all these particles some method of determining their relationship to the space around themselves,* rather than to particles that are not near them.

"Inertia is also a matter of time. In order to have motion, you must have not only coordinates in space, but coordinates in time.

"It would seem that since inertia deals with the mass of an object, and its velocity, that what we may be dealing with is a shadow, or phase effect, wherein the object in the past instant sees its own image of a future instant as being in a particular direction in space.

"Thus, inertia could be defined as the strong gravity field of an object falling towards the future ghost of itself.

"Or we might equally postulate on the first law that the object is moving away from the ghost of itself in the past. Since two objects may not occupy the same space at the same time, it could be that one object will repel itself from its own former ghost.

"However we phrase it, it adds up to the same thing —a memory oriented in space of the velocity and direction of motion of any mass.

"Communication between particles by any means is apparently limited by the speed of light, which is a relationship between space and time; but apparently, from what we know of inertia, if the universe contained only a single particle, and that particle was in motion, it would continue to move regardless of the fact that its motion could not be checked upon in relation to other particles.

"This indicates to me that the particle has an existence in space because it is created out of space, and that space must, therefore, have some very real properties of its own regardless of what is or is not in it. The very fact that there is a limiting speed to light and particle motion introduces the concept that space has physical properties.

"In order to have an electromagnetic wave, one must have a medium in which an electric field or a magnetic field can exist. In order to have matter, which I believe to be a form of electromagnetic field in stasis, one must have special properties which make the existence of matter possible. In order to have inertia, one must also have spatial properties which make the existence of inertia possible.

"People are fond of pointing out that there's nothing to get hold of in free space in order to climb the ladder of gravity, or in order to move between planets, and that the only possibility of motion of a vehicle in space is to throw something away, or, in other words, to lose mass in order to gain speed by reaction. Which is simply a statement that as far as we can tell a force can only be exerted relative to two points—or between two points or masses.

"But this does not account for the continuance of motion once started.

"Inertia says a body will move once started, but it doesn't say why or how. How does that particle once started gain the knowledge to continue without some direct control over its spatial framework? That it will continue, we know. That in the presence of a gravitic field or a magnetic field or other attractive force at right angles to its motion, we can create an acceleration which will maintain it in a circular path called an orbit. But how does it remember, as soon as that field ceases to exist, where it was going before it was last influenced? That it will continue in a straight line indefinitely, without such an influence, we know. That it can be influenced over a distance by various field effects, we also know. But what is the mechanism of influence whereby it influences itself to continue in a straight line? And what handle did we get hold of to convert that influence of self to our own advantage in moving this ship?"

Mike stared at Ishie with vast respect.

"I thought you physics boys did it all with math," he said softly, "and here you've outlined the facts of space that an Indian can feel in his bones—and you've done it in good, solid English that makes sense."

Then he shook himself like a dog coming out of water.

"Oh, well," he said. "Anyway, we've got a space drive —flea-sized. Now the question before the board becomes, just what are we going to do with it? Turn it over to the captain?"

"Confusion say," said Ishie, "that he who has very little is often most generous. But he who has huge fortune is cautious about dispersing it. Let's first be sure what we've got," he grinned slyly at Mike, "before we become over-generous with information."

Mike heaved a sigh of relief. He had been afraid he would have to argue Ishie into this point of view.

"Speaking of math, Mike, you're no slouch at it yourself, if you figured out all those orbit coordinates in your head, and arrived at an exact figure on the amount of thrust. It would be very nice for our future investigations if we had some method of putting the Cow to work on this."

The little physicist sat back, grinned knowingly, and continued: "Where's your secret panel, Mike? We've got to keep this information from going to anyone else."

"Oh, I already. . . ." Mike stopped. "I mean," he floundered, "Uh . . . how did you know?" A foolish smile spread over his face. "It's right behind you," he said. "And I've got it by voice," he added proudly. "Just push the switch in the corner and talk to it."

Ishie turned, glanced at the panel, went over to the switch and pushed it. "I wondered how you were concealing the teletype," he said. "You mean you really talk to it?"

The Sacred Cow's voice came back. "Reference not understood. Please explain."

"Oh," said Ishie. "It even sounds like a cow!"

"Yes, sir," said the Cow. "A cow is an herbivorous animal, usually domesticated, and found in most of the countries of Earth. What specific data did you wish? The milk supply——"

"Hold it," Mike said, forestalling a long dissertation on the dairy industry.

Catching on quickly to the literal-mindedness of the placid computer, Ishie fired a direct question.

"What is our current position in relation to the equatorial orbit that we should be following?" he asked.

There was a *sputt* from the speaker, very much as though someone had been caught off-guard and almost said something, and then the placid reply came back. "That information is top secret. Please identify yourself as Mike and I will answer you."

Ishie groaned, depressed the cutoff switch, and turned to Mike.

"You fixed it," he said. "If a simple question like that

gets an answer like that, how long do you think it will take the captain to find out something's wrong with the Cow?"

Mike lunged for the switch, but Ishie held him back.

"Hold it, there," he said. "You've made enough electronic mistakes for one day. This takes some thinking over."

"We better think fast," said Mike. "The captain's bound to ask that question first thing, or a question like it."

"All right," said Ishie. "First we've got to withdraw your original order—and you'd better not trust your own memory as to what it was. You ask the Cow to tell you what order you gave her making certain information top secret. Then when she tells you exactly what you said, you tell her to cancel *that* order."

Mike did as he was told.

"Why," asked Ishie, "did you give such an order in the first place? Never mind answering that question," he added, "but it's lucky she hasn't been refusing to give people the time of day, and referring them to you. As a matter of fact," glancing up at the clock on the wall, "it looks like she has. That clock hasn't moved since I got here."

Even as he spoke, the clock whirred, jumped forty-five minutes, and settled down to its steady second-by-second spin.

"Ishie," said Mike, "we figured out a space drive, and that was great. But if we can figure out how to communicate an idea to a computer, we're *real* geniuses."

Ishie turned on the vocoder. "Please supply us," he told the Cow, "with a complete recording of your latest conversation with Mike."

The computer started back over the dialogue that had just occurred between herself and Mike, and Ishie inter-

114

rupted hastily. "Not that one," he said, with a wry grimace, "I mean the last previous conversation."

Then he sat back as the Cow unreeled a fifteen minute monologue which repeated both sides of the conversation including the order to make everything top secret.

Having listened through this, Ishie said; "At the point where Mike asks you about acceleration, you will now erase the rest of the conversation and substitute this comment from yourself: 'The lab is being accelerated by an external magneto-ionic effect.' This will be your only explanation of the acceleration applied to the ship, and will be given to anyone who queries you. Now please repeat your conversation with Mike."

Then he sat back to listen through the recording again.

This time when it came to the part about acceleration, without hesitation the Cow blithely referred to the external magneto-ionic effect that was causing that acceleration.

Then Ishie asked the computer: "How could this effect be cancelled?" and listened to a long syllogistic outline which, if condensed to a single, understandable sentence meant simply "By reversing the field in respect to the ship with a magnet on board the ship."

Ishie heaved a great sigh of relief, and said, "Now, Mike, we can go to work. For of course," he added, "we must have authority to install our magnetic coils, and what better authority is there than the Cow?"

Then he added, "Confusion say it is better to have the voice of authority speak with your words than to be the voice of authority.

"Now, let us see what we have really got here."

As they worked, the empty racks around the Confusor slowly filled with more test instruments, both borrowed and devised; and the formerly unoccupied corner of the section of panels took on more and more the look of a complete installation, in the center of which the Confusor still churkled quietly, pitting its strength against the mighty monster to which it was so firmly tied.

Nearly two hours were spent in testing circuits, each one exhaustively.

Captain Naylor Andersen arrived on the bridge with an accusing air, but feeling refreshed. He had slept longer than he intended—and though he had asked Bessie to call him when she came back on duty two hours earlier, he had not been called.

"You needed the sleep, Captain," she told him, unrepentant. "I checked with the Cow. The flare's predicted to continue for another eight hours. We're simply in standby."

At his console, Clark murmured into the private channel the information that the captain was on the bridge. Almost immediately the official teletype from U.N. Headquarters began to chatter. It was not a long message, and Clark tore it off, placed it on top of the pile of innocuous material that had arrived earlier, and presented the pile to the captain.

"There was nothing that seemed to me of sufficient importance to disturb you earlier, sir. But I imagine this last that just arrived. . . ." He left the sentence hanging and went back to his console.

The captain picked the sheet from the top of the pile and read quickly through it.

"Tracking stations report your orbital discontinuity too great to have been achieved by jet action of nitrogen escaping from HOT ROD. HOT ROD pressures insufficient to achieve your present apparent acceleration. Also, discontinuity is in the wrong direction for HOT ROD to

116

be source. Please explain discrepancy between these reports and your own summation of ten hours previous. Suspect, repeat, strongly suspect, possibility of sabotage. Was destruction of Thule Base intentional query. End message."

Nails Andersen stared at the sheet of paper in his hand with a sickening sense of unreality.

But the sentence continued to stare back at him. *"Was the destruction of Thule Base intentional. . . ."*

VIII

Nails Andersen thrust the offending sheet of paper from him, together with the sense of unreality it engendered. A coil of anger replaced his momentary shock.

What form of idiot do they think we are up here, he asked himself; then brought his attention back to the problem of finding out just exactly what situation existed that could cause the hardboiled men of U.N. Headquarters to make such far-flung assumptions. A disaster of the proportions of the destruction of Thule Base could cause men to go temporarily paranoic, he decided, even as he spoke to Bessie.

"Get an orbit computation from the Cow, as rapidly as possible, for the time since the flare. Have it displayed against a graph of our programmed orbit," he said fiercely, then dialed the intercom to the morgue.

"Dr. Kimball. Report to the bridge. Dr. P.E.R. Kimball, report to the bridge immediately!"

Under Bessie's practiced, computer-minded fingers, computations and graphs came almost by the time he had finished speaking into the intercom. The screens displayed a string of figures, each to three decimal places, accompanied by a second display on the captain's console showing the old equatorial orbit across a grid projection of the Earth's surface to a point of departure over the mid-Atlantic where it began curving ever farther north, up across the tip of South America, very slightly off course.

The captain glanced at the display and then at the display of HOT ROD on its taut cable that had been kept on the console screen since the disaster so that the duty officers could keep a check on the balloon. He realized with a sinking feeling of dismay that no jet action on HOT ROD could have caused it to lead the station in this northerly direction, that instead it was tranquilly trailing behind. It was now further south of the Space Lab than its original position, but the orbit of the complex had been displaced to the north.

Perk appeared beside the console, but the captain ignored the astronomer for a moment longer, while he leaned back thinking. What could be the answer? What —whether caused by natural or human agency—could have given the wheel this off-orbit acceleration? A leak in the Space Lab itself? That would give acceleration, minor, not to have triggered an alarm—or a saboteur could have silenced an alarm. Acceleration sufficient for the off-orbit shown? He did a brief calculation in his head. It wouldn't take much. Very little, for the time that had passed. Very well, then. He put down a leak in his mind as a possibility. Now, water or air? It could be either, if his reasoning this far were correct. He looked up.

"Have the Cow display barometric readings for each section of the rim and for each compartment in the central hub," he said to Bessie; and to the astronomer, "Dr. Kimball, take that side seat at the computer console and check our progress on this orbital deviation," and he gestured at the display on his screen.

Perk moved to the post with only a nod.

The barometric displays held constant, with only fractional deviations that might have been imposed by the spin of the big wheel, or error in the instruments themselves. Balanced against temperature readings, they worked out to possible fractions of gain or loss so small as to be insignificant, indicating only the inaccuracies of measurement that inevitably occur in comparing the readings of a number of instruments.

The captain had hardly digested the readings displayed by the computer when Perk looked up with a puzzled frown.

"The computer records a continuous acceleration over the past eleven hours and forty-three minutes," he said puzzled, "and attributes it to a magneto-ionic effect?" There was a definite question in his voice. He added, "It's only about six hundred forty pounds. It must be an external effect caused by the flare."

"Investigate the effect as thoroughly as possible," the captain told Perk, then leaned back in his chair.

He'd have to message Earth quickly, he knew. The magneto-ionic effect? The Cow had vast information that was pedantically accurate. Why hadn't he asked the Cow last night? But this was no time for self-recrimination. The ship was suspect, and that was intolerable. Headquarters would undoubtedly confine such suspicions to the higher echelons of their own personnel, preventing any such suspicion from leaking to the public. Even so, it could have widespread political repercussions just from that small coterie itself. It must not be allowed to continue.

U.N. Headquarters was not, however, given to jump-

ing to conclusions. Was it possible that there was a saboteur aboard? Was it even an outside possibility?

He went over the conditions that had existed from the
moment of the flare alarm in his mind. Was it possible
that a magneto-ionic effect could have been caused by
human agency? That as the crew responded to the flare
alarm, some possible subversive had triggered a pre-set
method for making the ship respond to the vast magnetic
and ionic disturbances outside?

"Ask the Cow whether the ship's response to the magnetic and ionic effects outside could have been triggered
by human agency," he said to Bessie, his voice controlled
but with a fury beneath that triggered her fingers to
rapid work.

Bessie turned shortly. "The effect is external to the
ship, sir. The computer replies only that the effect is
external to the ship."

I'm going to have to have somebody who understands
such an effect, Nails told himself. But first I'd better take
some measures against the possibility that sabotage is
involved. Not intentional destruction of Thule—not possibly. But sabotage. . . .

He dialed the morgue. What had been that Security
officer's name? Chauvenseer. "Chauvenseer. Report to the
bridge."

The officer reached the bridge fairly quickly, and saluted smartly as he entered. "Yes, Captain?"

"Select four of your best men. Station them . . . well,
two each at the north and south entrances to the rim from
the hub. They can be stationed well inside the shield area,
and still command the passenger entrances. No one is to
leave the hub," he said. Then he added, "This is for your
information only, not to be repeated to the men nor to
anyone except those on the bridge. Earth suspects sabotage

in last night's disaster. Have your men report any unusual actions, as well as anyone attempting to get to the
rim . . . or to any post outside the flare shield area itself." Then he smiled grimly. "It would be worth a man's
life to leave the shield area, so I don't personally expect
such an attempt. However, your men will see to it that it
does not occur."

As the Security officer departed, Nails dialed the morgue
again. "Dr. Chi," he said. "Please report to the bridge.
Dr. Chi Tung. Please report to the bridge at once."

The intercom came alive at the far end, and a voice
came on. "Dr. Chi Tung is not in the morgue, Captain.
He left with Mr. Blackhawk some time ago."

The captain frowned, but dialed the engineering room
intercom.

Meantime, in the engineering compartment, Ishie had
nearly satisfied himself with the conclusions he could
reach with the various tests he and Mike had applied.
But he wasn't totally satisfied. "We need still another
test that we have not provided," he said after a moment's
thought. "A strain gauge to find out how much thrust a
mosquito can put out. There's one in the physics lab.
I'll run get it."

"You will *not*," said Mike. "Genius you may be, but
proton-proof you're not. We can rig that right here."

Walking over to the spare parts locker, Mike brought
back a complete readout display panel, a spare one from
the Cow's bridge consoles; and quickly connected it into
the data link on which the vocoder operated. Then, carefully instructing the computer as to the required display,
he settled back.

"That'll do it," he said. "The Cow can tell us all we
need to know right on that panel—about acceleration,

lack of it, or change of it that we may cause by changing the parameters of our experiment. Those racks were checked out to stand up under eighty gees," he added. "Typical overspecification. They never said what would happen to the personnel under those conditions."

Ishie turned the Confusor off and then back on, and watched the display gauge rise to the six hundred forty mark, and then show the fraction above it, .12128. Then carefully, ever so infinitesimally, he adjusted a knob on the device. The readout sank back towards zero, coming to rest reading 441.3971.

"We'll have to put a vernier control on this phase circuit," Ishie said to himself. "It jumped thirty percent, and I scarcely breathed on it."

After a few more checks on the operation of the phase control, he turned to the power control for the magnetic field. Carefully, Ishie lowered the field strength, eye on the readout panel. As the field strength lowered, the reading increased.

The indication was that by lowering the field strength only ten percent, he had increased the thrust to sixteen hundred pounds—which, he felt, was close to the tolerance of the machine structure.

Carefully he increased the field strength again. Faithfully the reading followed it down the scale.

Then he had another thought. Running the field strength down and the pressure up, and again arriving at sixteen hundred pounds, he turned off the Confusor, waited a few moments, and turned it back on.

The reading remained zero.

Apparently, then, a decrease in field strength would cause an increase in thrust; but the original field strength was necessary in order to initiate the thrust field.

Carefully he nudged the field strength back up, and

suddenly there were seven hundred ten pounds indicated thrust.

Thrust could apparently be initiated by a field strength a few percent lower, but not much lower, than the original operating point.

The captain's voice came over the intercom: "Mr. Blackhawk. Is Dr. Chi with you?"

"Yes he is, Captain. Right here."

"Will you both report to the bridge, please?"

When the two arrived, only a little tardily, the captain addressed himself to Ishie, and while Mike watched the small, wizened face which had seemed that of a bad boy or a leprechaun metamorphosed into that of a frail Chinese sage.

The guy changes to fit the people around him, Mike thought in awe. The scholar whom the captain was addressing was a far cry from the conspirator with whom he had been working for the past two hours.

But the captain was speaking. "You heard of the disaster last night?" There was something about the captain's voice that disturbed Mike—a note of fierce anger, controlled fury.

The physicist nodded.

"We assumed at that time," the captain continued, "that a meteor had caused the disaster; that it had gone through the balloon making a hole through which the balloon's nitrogen was escaping, causing jet reaction and accelerating the ship.

"It seems, however, that—according to the computer— we are under acceleration from what it terms an external magneto-ionic effect. Can you tell me what such an effect would be, whether this sounds reasonable to you, and how it could affect the ship?"

"Magneto-ionic. . . . Why, yes, Captain. That could

very well be. Why had we not considered the possibility beforehand? You see, in a solar flare, the solar wind becomes charged with——of course, the X-rays come first, and then come the protons——highly ionized particles, which are sweeping out in such a way as to warp the various overlapping magnetic fields, which include the sun's own field and the various planets——"

The captain interrupted. "It is possible then that such an effect could affect the ship's orbit?"

"Highly probable, I'd think; highly probable. You see, the magnetic effects——of course I'd have to check the mathematics——but the magnetic effects combined with the sweeping flood of——"

"I shall not take up your time, Dr. Chi, with trying to explain electromagnetics to a layman. However, since the computer insists, and you confirm, that this effect could be the influencing factor on the ship's orbit. . . . Mr. Blackhawk, could a deviation of the ship's orbit have thrown HOT ROD off her communications beam and caused last night's disaster?"

"I guess I'd have to check by math, too, captain. . . ." Mike appeared to debate the question. "It would be a very small acceleration at first, of course," he said solemnly, "from only six hundred forty pounds of thrust. But the motion increases as the square of the time—— and HOT ROD's cable is normally slack. The velocity needn't have been great to deliver quite a jolt when the slack was taken up——lever effect, you know. Yes, I feel quite sure *that* could happen, Captain."

"Very well." The captain paused, then continued with a deliberately noncommittal voice. "Now, Dr. Chi. Could a human agency in any way have caused the ship's response to the magneto-ionic effect?"

It burst from each of them simultaneously. "Human agency?"

"I mean, of course, *intentional* human agency." The captain's voice was grim. "I am asking whether it is possible that a saboteur is responsible for the ship's erratic behaviour and its effects. Whether it is at all possible that a saboteur could have been the cause of the destruction of Thule Base."

Mike was stopped. He couldn't lie on that one. He and Ishie *had* been responsible—or rather, he had, he told himself firmly—but they weren't saboteurs. Though they'd never be able to prove the fact.

But Ishie was answering, and his voice was grave. "Captain, I do not believe that a saboteur could have or would have—*intentionally*—caused last night's disaster. Acceleration applied to the ship, whether by intent or by accident, would have that disaster as an improbable rather than a predictable result. True, HOT ROD was programmed for a spot north of Thule. But any intentional usage of the lever effect caused by the acceleration would have been predicated on the ability to predict results— and with as many variables as you would have concerned in such a random setup, prediction would have been quite impossible. It was just as probable that the beam would have swept through the Atlantic ocean, for instance; or confined itself to the spot on the ice cap to which it had been programmed—if, indeed, the balloon responded by turning on at all.

"No, Captain, I do not think that anyone with the intention of accomplishing anything of any disastrous nature would possibly have chosen this means. Even if they could have so chosen it—which seems highly doubtful as well. It *is* possible," he added slowly, "that some accidental action by a human being could have initiated the series of events by which the disaster was caused. But intent? No, Captain, you can rule that out."

The captain relaxed visibly. "Thank you, Dr. Chi," he said. "Thank you for the completeness of your outline. It follows my own thinking. However, Earth suspects sabotage, sir. And I must, of course, eliminate that possibility first—along with the necessity to eliminate the current effect on the ship's orbit, or the recurrence of such an effect. Even with your analysis I must continue to guard against the possibility of a saboteur, remote though such a possibility may be.

"However, that need not concern you. Dr. Chi, is there any manner in which the effect on the ship can be nullified? And its recurrence prevented?"

Ishie's voice was not as sure as it had been, and some of the vitality seemed to have oozed from the small physicist as he talked. But he answered firmly, "I believe I can design a means for countering the effect. And preventing its accidental recurrence. I will start work immediately, designing such a means."

"Please do, and report to me as soon as you have anything concrete at all. I will then submit your theories to the other scientists aboard that may have some selective knowledges in the field, and to Earth. You may, of course, call on any of the personnel aboard ship for assistance, and possibly Mr. Blackhawk may be of assistance to you. He is familiar with the design of the ship and its equipment."

The captain paused, then cleared his throat. "You probably recognize the urgency for speed in your solution, so I shall not attempt to underline that urgency further, except to ask whether it is possible that countering measures can be designed and constructed before our orbital deviation becomes disastrous in itself? If not, it may become necessary to make successive orbit corrections with rockets." His voice held the pain of potential Budget Control hearings. "Please give me a time estimate as soon as that becomes possible."

Mike heard a soft kindness in Ishie's answer that metamorphosed the tiny physicist again into the wise philosopher reassuring a neophyte. "It should not take more than a couple of hours to design—countermeasures—with the information I already have," he said, "and not too long to construct the means to put them into effect. You need not fear having to abandon ship, Captain."

When the two had left, Nails returned to his console and dictated a message to Earth.

"Original assumption that disaster was attributable to meteoric impact on Project HOT ROD mistaken. Investigation indicates that we are under acceleration from an external magneto-ionic effect which is exerting about . . ." He turned to Perk, still at the computer's console, "Was that an exact thrust of six hundred forty pounds?"

"No, sir," replied the astronomer. "It was a fraction over."

". . . is exerting a little over six hundred forty pounds pressure against this satellite, apparently in a northerly direction. Computer confirms assumption that this pressure is the acceleration factor. Am not disregarding your suspicion of sabotage, but find it highly unlikely due to the fact that the results of such sabotage would have been unpredictable, that all personnel have been confined to the flare shield area since approximately two hours before the disaster, and that it seems unlikely in the extreme that any of the personnel aboard Lab I could have or would have intentionally precipitated such an act of war even if it were possible. Such an action, even if possible, could not be even partially effective without the cooperation of all personnel aboard, especially the captain. However, the strictest investigation will be instigated immediately, and security measures taken on the possibility that such a likelihood could exist. If you know any factors other than that of the laboratory's orbital discontinuity on which to base such an assumption, please message immediately. Meanwhile, measures to counteract the much more logical, and computer-confirmed, likelihood of a magneto-ionic effect are being worked out. End message."

Chad Clark kept the satisfaction he felt internally from showing on his face as he transcripted the message to Earth. That bit about its needing the captain's cooperation was perfect, he thought.

Then he activated the private wire. "The flare effect is clearing a bit," he told the voice at the other end. "I can already get nearly intelligible voices by radio."

"We will put up a jamming beam, directed on the Lab, immediately," the voice answered.

"And—if I may suggest, sir?—keep up a demand for that saboteur-hunt. The captain doesn't believe there is a saboteur, but the possibility is forcing him to place our men where we are going to need to have them."

IX

In the engineering quarters the two conspirators remained only momentarily subdued.

"It *wasn't* intentional, Mike." Ishie was reassuring himself more than his cohort. "And we have given the world a space drive. We could wish the price had not been so high—but, Mike, we have taken the stopper out of the bottle, and mankind need not explode in his own steam. We even have permission to construct a real drive.

"Now," he continued, his momentary guilt falling from him, "Confusion say he who can fly on wings of mosquito fly better on wings of eagle. How much thrust do we want?"

"What are our limits?" asked the practical engineer.

"Limits, schlimits. We got *power*. Of course," he added, "we *are* limited by the acceptable stress limits on the wheel and, yes, by the stress limits of our plastic, too."

"The wheel was designed to stand upwards of 1.5 gee maximum spin—but that's only radial strength." Mike began figuring. "I don't think anybody ever calculated the stress of pulling the hub loose, endwise. No reason to, you know. It wasn't expected to land or anything. And really, nobody expected it to stand in service more than 1.5 gee spin on the rim. They computed these racks to take all kinds of shock, but the overall structure is rather flimsily built." He paused for thought. "We could maybe put a tenth of a gee on the axis, but I better check some of the stress figures against the structural pattern with the Cow first. We'll have to give some thought to strengthening things later, if we really want to go into the fantastic possibility of landing this monster anywhere."

Consulted, the Sacred Cow computed a potential maximum of stress-safety at the hub of something over two-tenths of a gee, and the two finally settled on one-tenth as well within the limits.

"Now the other limit," said Ishie. "This little piece of plastic will only stand a pressure approaching the point at which it begins to distort and run out of the field. This stuff is quoted to have a compression-yield strength of one hundred ten pounds to the square inch. We probably shouldn't exceed . . . hmmm . . . ninety pounds. Let's get the Cow to tell us how big a chunk of surface area that represents."

The answer was discouraging. Mike rapidly converted the figure in centimeters to feet, and came up with nearly an eighty-three foot diameter for a circular surface.

"Looks like we'll have to put it out on the spokes," he muttered in disgust, but Ishie shook his head quickly.

"No need, Mike. Later on we'll need a few thrust points out on the rim for good aiming, but we don't have to have all this surface area in one unit or even in one place. Also, we do not need to consider only the surface of an homogenous piece of plastic material.

"This plastic can be cast. Very easily. In it, we can insert structures that will absorb the strain from many surfaces within, rather than only on a front surface."

Glass thread reinforcing the plastic was the available answer to that they decided—and came up against the problem of a parallel magnetic field. "To get an absolutely parallel field, the gap between the pole faces can't be very wide," Mike objected.

"Perhaps I wasn't considering pole faces," Ishie answered. "Our investigation has already shown that once initiated, the thrust-effect works best in a very low magnetic field. . . ."

A solenoid would supply that field, they found; and the strong field needed to initiate the action could be external to the plastic. Testing, they found it took a one thousand microsecond pulse to initiate thrust, but that the solenoid carried it easily thereafter.

Mike sat back. "Okay," he said, "it's going to look like a barrel with a hump on its back. And we get one-tenth gee thrust. Cumulative, per second per second. Take a few hours to get up to speed, but then we ought to race along nicely, building as we go . . . towards light speeds. . . .

"I wish," he added wistfully, "that we could get one point one gee. And land this thing on Earth. And have a big parade, with Space Lab I hovering just overhead to the cheers and the blaring bands and the——"

"Confusion say, he who would poke hole in hornets' nest had best be prepared with long legs." Ishie grinned. "You don't think anybody would really appreciate our doing that, do you Mike? Outside of the people themselves, that is, that aren't directly concerned with man's *welfare?* We haven't done this in the proper manner of team research and billions spent in experiments and planned predicted achievements made with the proper Madison Avenue bow to the corporation that made it possible. You know what they do to wild-haired individualists down there, don't you?"

Mike shrugged. "Oh, well," he said, "you're right of course. But it was a beautiful dream. How do you suppose we can build these and still keep all the scientists aboard and on Earth happy that they're just innocent magneto-ionic effect cancellers? Boy, that was a beauty, Ishie!"

"Best we have two sets of drawings. The ones for us can be sketchy, and need not have too much exactitude of design. We know what we're doing—at least I hope we do.

"But let us make a second set of drawings that is somewhat different, though of a similar shape and design, on which the other scientists aboard can speculate, and which can be sent to Earth to confuse the confusion."

The two went to work with a will, and as the two sets of drawings emerged, they were indeed different. The set from which they would actually work could be described only mildly as sketchy. The papers looked like the notations a man makes for himself to get the figures he will set into a formalized pattern as it takes shape, before throwing his pencilled figurings into the wastebasket.

The second set was exact, made with proper drawing instruments on Mike's drafting board, and each of the component circuits would have created an effect that would have interlocked into the whole, but it would take the most erudite of persons to figure each into its effect, and its effect into the whole, and the effect of the whole was something that somebody might someday figure out —but would possibly cancel a magneto-ionic effect if such existed. These drawings looked extremely impressive.

As the second set of drawings neared completion, Ishie glanced at the clock and then turned to the Cow's vocoder.

"How soon will Space Lab I reach the northernmost point of her present orbit and begin a swing to the south?" he asked.

Mike looked puzzled, but the Cow answered, "In ten minutes, thirty-seven seconds. At precisely 05:27:53 ship time."

"I think," said Ishie, "we'd best put a switch in our magnetic field so that we can reverse the field and the thrust."

"Why?" asked Mike.

"Because," Ishie explained, "when we reach the top of our course northward, then the thrust of the Confusor and Earth's gravity come into conflict, moving our entire orbit off-center and bringing us closer to the pole. In not too many orbits, that eccentricity in our orbit might pull us into the Van Allen belts. The captain was right, you know. He would have to change us by rockets. It would be much better if that didn't have to happen. Now, if we reverse the thrust at the right time, our orbit will be enlarged, and we stay out of troubled spaces."

Mike was still puzzled. "I don't see how that works," he said. "Why wouldn't we just go off in a spiral on our present thrust?"

"The acceleration of Earth is a much greater influence than our little mosquito here," Ishie tried to make it clear. "As long as they work together, things go well. But when Earth dictates that we will now swing south, be it ever so few degrees south, our mosquito is overpowered and can only drag us clear to Earth-center on a closing spiral, which would eventually lead us to crash somewhere in the southern hemisphere, a good many orbits from now.

"I hope," he said, "reversing the magnetic field will indeed reverse our little mosquito's thrust." He moved toward the Confusor.

"Hold it," said Mike. "The displacement in orbit won't be very much, at least on the first few go-arounds, will it? And if we switch it now, somebody'll start getting suspicious of this magneto-ionic effect. The effect that's doing all this. A sudden reversal might not be in its character, if it had a character. And anyhow, we don't want to give another jerk on HOT ROD. We might jerk something loose this time. We've already wiped out Thule Base—and there's no use adding scalps to an already full belt."

"Okay," said Ishie. "Then now, I think it is time that we presented our formal drawings to the captain; and I think that when we present them we will suggest that we start immediately on construction, even while he is checking out our drawings through his experts, so that the project shall not be delayed."

The captain received the formal set of drawings with an expression of intense relief. "Thank you, gentlemen," he said. "You have indeed worked rapidly. If these drawings prove to hold the answer, how long will it take to actually effect the cancellation? Earth is demanding results with quite inexplicable arbitrariness, and perhaps rightly so. Dr. Kimball calculates that our present acceleration, unless the deviation is corrected by rockets of which we have a limited supply, will take us dangerously close to the Van Allen belts within about six orbits."

"In that case, perhaps we should begin construction of the . . . cancelling device . . . without waiting for the results of your checks with the other scientists aboard and on Earth?" Ishie's voice was unperturbed. "If we start immediately, we should be able to produce what is needed, possibly in one orbit—not more than two, certainly."

"Of course," said the captain. "What assistance will you need?"

"Of the greatest priority," replied Ishie gravely, "is access to the machine shop. The proton storm should be about wearing itself out."

"The prediction is for several hours more of above-normal readings—Bessie, ask the computer for the exact M.R."

"Yes, sir." And shortly, "The computer says the radiation count is down to ten M.R. above normal."

"That's not too high." The captain thought a moment. "I'll have to return the entire ship to normal conditions to give the machine shop or any other part of the rim its regular six-foot shielding. But ten M.R. above should be safe enough. Bessie, start the count-down for a return of the shielding and personnel to the rim."

The return to the rim was slower than had been the evacuation—but it was complete within twenty minutes of the decision to return the ship to normal.

In the machine shop, Paul and Tombu, with Ishie and Mike, were gathering the materials they'd need for the odd construction. Paul sang to himself as he worked.

I got in the shuttle, thought it went to the Base
I'd learned me a trade; there I'd take my place
Safely on Earth; but I found me in space—
I'd went where I wasn't going!

"What's that song?" asked Ishie.

"Oh, that's just *The Spaceman's Lament*. You make it up as you go along." His voice grew louder, taking the minor, wailing key at a volume the others could hear.

I got on the wheel, thought I'd stay for the ride
I'd found a funny suit in which to hide—
But I went through a closet—and I was outside—
I'd went where I wasn't going!

Tombu and Mike joined happily in the chorus, bawling it out at the top of their lungs as they began the work that would make the big Confusor.

Oh . . . there's a sky-trail leading from here to there
And another yonder showing—
But when I get to the end of the run
It'll be where I wasn't going!

Meanwhile, facsimile copies of the official drawings had been made for the other interested scientists aboard, and also sent by transfax to U.N. Headquarters labelled for distribution among Earth's top level scientists.

They were innocent enough in concept, and sufficiently complex in interrelated design to require a great deal of study by these conservative individuals who would never risk a hasty guess as to the consequences of even so simple an action as sneezing at the wrong time, much less the audacity necessary to the hazard of defying the conclusions of the eminent Dr. Chi.

Meantime, too, in response to pressures from Earth,

the captain had stationed Security officers outside eac
laboratory, and had even retained two of the four he ha
originally placed in the central axis tube of the hub.

On Earth the giant machine that had been readie
long before had gone into action. It was a machine mad
up of movies and sounds; of prepared military comman
ders and unprepared civilian officials; of shock effect an
skilled propaganda herding; of simultaneous actions i
planet-wide patterns along detailed lines long since keye
to instant operation towards predetermined effects. It wa
a masterminded, all-mediums-included, total militar
coup.

It was technological overkill that had been ready an
waiting, and was now executed with button-pushing aut
maticity. It had been prepared with the most advance
scientific, sociological and military techniques, combinin
the traditions of Madison Avenue with the overt action
of a military occupying force. It was oriented to a civili
zation that had not yet recognized its own dependenc
upon and Pavlovian reactions to its automated "servants.

The originating roots of the total coup could hav
been found in the evolution of control over the elector:
process of democracies which had culminated in the earl
'70s. The skills of this operation, however, went far be
yond those first, inept roots.

The initiating action was a catastrophe commandin
attention and creating confusion. That the catastrophe ha
been accidental rather than intentional changed nothin
except the initiating moment.

From the original rumor of a space disaster, it ha
become known that a tremendous accident had wiped ou
Thule Base and left a smoking ruins of Greenland.

From this it had become "possible sabotage." At th:

moment, the military forces could move. "Subversives" were rounded up and long-prepared concentration camps opened to receive them. That the "subversives" lists, constantly updated and in the hands of the units that would arrest and confine them, were actually lists of leaders of any and every stamp and variety, there was no opportunity for the public to discover.

Only enough time for the "subversives" to be rousted out and rounded up—a matter of a couple of hours— was allowed to elapse before every news media was fed word that the scientists of Space Lab I were to make a broadcast shortly, and that the military *suspected* that Thule had been a direct, unprovoked attack by those scientists on Earth itself. "A mad act, but increasingly evident as new information was received," the military was quoted as saying in direct release, and in "leaks" the words were even stronger.

Then, abruptly, the movie was broadcast, playing as a direct broadcast from the satellite—and almost every TV screen across the planet was tuned in.

The scene showed Nails Andersen in uniform, at the command console of the big wheel, making demands in the name of the "new space people."

The voice demeaned Earth and its problems as unworthy of respect, abrogated to the ship above their heads and its peoples the right to control Earth, to be supported by Earth in a vast program of subservience and thralldom.

The men who had created the greatest weapon the world had ever known, its peoples were told, were prepared to use that weapon as often and as severely as necessary until Earth learned. . . .

The scene shifted and showed the scientists of the laboratory clapping and cheering at the words; shifted again to show Security guards locked into an empty laboratory where they had been placed when taken in a surprise move; shifted yet again to show the weapon that had wiped out Thule, and that could and would be used again as often as necessary.

Then it showed, in detail, the ruins that once were Thule.

A race of superpeople had been created, the captain's voice assured "his subject peoples" and although their rights would be considered, the demands of the space people would at all times be met.

As the screen blanked from the space ship, it shifted to the halls of the U.N. Assembly, where statesman after statesman was standing forth, condemning actions of country after country that had made possible the great wheel.

Then the podium was taken by a military figure.

Earth would be protected, it announced. The U.N. would act through its Security Forces, and those forces would not be helpless.

Security, it was discovered—and the discovery was cheered—could and was reactivating the majority of all weapons that it had so boastingly told everyone had been scrapped; security could and would reactivate—in hours—the majority of all stockpiles of ships and planes and ammunition, all the secretly built extra shuttles and space paraphernalia.

Even now, Security shuttles with armies aboard and sufficient weapons, were being readied for launch into the Space Lab orbit.

The military figure assured the people, Security had the manpower to put the defense of Earth into operation. Its numbers, supposedly small, were rapidly updated to show great armies, navies and air force personnel, "readied for an emergency—such an emergency as has occurred."

The honeyed phrases which had assured there would always be peace on Earth because the means of making war had been destroyed, were all forgotten now, and changed, and the individual nations were forgotten as well.

Now, it was the U.N. that was the military power—and that power resided in the hands of U.N. Security, in which the people could trust.

Mobilization must be declared. A war footing established for the economy. Everyone must fight back against the insane scientists above with their inhuman weapon.

With appalling swiftness, where apparently nothing had been before, a military force had stepped forth in full armor to grind man's hopes for freedom under an iron heel while waving its fist at the stars.

And the voices that might have had the temerity to speak out, even under these circumstances, had almost totally been silenced behind the guarded barbed wire barriers of concentration camps, easily found and placed there by forces whose teams had kept the lengthy lists of people under surveillance for weeks in readiness for the action.

Even so, there were scattered voices crying out against the monstrous action, but the broadcast media were preempted and their effect localized. Even where they were heard, the threat from above was too real, too terrifying, and the voices had slowly been softened, spotted and removed, or been ignored.

Within hours, the question involved had come to a vote—and the vote only failed of being unanimous by one abstention.

War was declared. U.N. Security Forces were granted dictatorial powers . . . For the "duration of the emergency."

The die was cast, and the yoke fitted ever so snugly but firmly across mankind's back, while he cheered the fitting.

X

Space Lab I floated among the last tenuous veils of the storm of protons that had passed her, but bathed now in a jamming beam from Earth that effectively nullified any broadcast communications reception.

Her scientists, still somewhat shaken by the horrifying accident that they were assured had resulted from the proton storm, waited patiently, assuming the lack of reception of further news to be the effect of that same storm. Meantime, they concerned themselves with reorganizing their laboratories from the effects of the forced evacuation.

In the hospital area of the morgue, Major Steve Elbertson woke with a start to see a medic's eyes only inches from his own. For a moment, fearing himself under physical attack, he struck out convulsively, and then as the face withdrew, he sat up slowly.

He was slightly nauseous; very dizzy; and his instincts told him that he needed a gallon of coffee as soon as he could get it. Then the medic's voice penetrated.

"Please, sir, you must rest. No excitement."

Almost, he was persuaded. It would be easy to relax;

to give someone else the responsibility. But the concept of responsibility brought him struggling up again.

HOT ROD was a dangerous weapon. He could *not* act irresponsibly.

"How long was I out?" he muttered.

The medic glanced at the clock. "Just over nineteen hours, sir."

"Wha-at? You dared to keep me off duty that long? I must get back immediately."

"Please, sir. No excitement. You must rest. Just a moment and I'll call Dr. Green." With that the medic turned and fled.

As Dr. Green approached, Steve Elbertson was already on his feet, swaying dizzily and white as a sheet, but perhaps the latter was more from anger than anything else.

"Major Elbertson. You received a severe dose of radiation. You are under my personal supervision and will return to bed at once."

"Is the flare over?" Elbertson asked the question, although already vaguely aware that the ship was again in her normal spin, that he was standing on the floor fairly firmly, and that, therefore, the emergency must be over.

"Yes."

"In that case, sir, my duty is to my post on HOT ROD."

"HOT ROD's out of commission and so are you. I cannot be responsible for the consequences if you do not follow my orders."

"Explain that. About HOT ROD, I mean."

"Why, it was struck by a meteor shortly after the flare last night. I think I heard someone say that it burned out Thule Base before they managed to turn it off."

Without waiting for more, Elbertson brushed past the doctor and headed for the bridge.

The captain was startled by the mad-eyed, unshaven, scarecrow of an officer that approached him, demanding in a near-scream, "What happened? What have you done? What did you do to Project HOT ROD? No one should have tampered with it without my direct order! Captain, if that mechanism has been ruined, I'll have them nail your hide to the door!"

"Major!" The captain stood. "This may be a civilian post, but you are still an officer and I am your superior. Return to your quarters and clean up. Then report to me properly!"

For a moment there was seething rebellion on Elbertson's already wild features. Then, like an automaton, he turned and walked stiffly away without saluting.

The stiffness left him as he passed through the door. Momentarily he sagged against a wall for support, far weaker than he had thought possible for a man of his age and what he thought of as his condition. Making his way almost blindly to Security's quarters in rim-section B-5, he staggered through the door and on towards the latrine, shouting at Chauvenseer to "Get out from behind that desk and give me a detailed report on events since the flare. Oh, and send somebody for coffee—lots of coffee."

On the bridge the captain dialed the intercom to Dr. Green's station. "Is Major Elbertson under the influence of any unusual drugs, Doctor?" he asked when he'd reached the medical staff chief. "Anything that might make his behavior erratic?"

"Only sedatives, Captain. And, oh yes, those new sulph-hydral anti-radiation shots. We're not too familiar with what they do, though the reports indicate the worst effect is a mild anoxemia, which generally results in something of a headache. Of course, that's if the quantity of the drug was precisely calibrated. They can be fatal," he added as an afterthought.

"Would anoxemia cause a change in character, Doctor?"

"It might. It might make one behave either stupidly or irrationally—temporarily or permanently, depending on the severity of the effect."

"Did Major Elbertson seem normal to you when you discharged him from the hospital?"

"I did not discharge him, Captain. I ordered him to remain under my care. But he seemed greatly upset, and short of force I could not have kept him from leaving."

"I see." The captain paused, then asked: "Doctor, please consider carefully. Would you consider Major Elbertson's condition serious enough to warrant confining him to bed by force?"

"Probably not. He should come out of it in a few hours. Exercise may possibly be good for him, though I doubt if he's capable of much of it." The doctor chuckled as though at a private joke with himself, then added, "He's really quite weak physically, you know, even without the aftereffects of radiation and drugs."

"Thank you, Doctor."

At his console, Chad Clark sat frozen. The C.O. was conscious, up and on duty. But had he gone crazy from the anti-radiation medication?—he didn't know.

But Chad Clark did know that he couldn't handle Operation Ripe Peach at this end himself. He was already groggy from almost twenty-four hours of duty, even if he had that type of command ability. Besides, suppose something went wrong? And he was next in real, though not in known, rank—for all that he was just a lieutenant.

No, he reassured himself. The C.O.'s just coming out of it, and he's under pressure, knowing he's been out. I'll give him half an hour, he thought. But what to report to Earth?

Cautiously keying the private channel, he told the voice on the far end: "Major Elbertson is beginning to come out of the dope they fed him. I will have him briefed in half an hour."

In his quarters, Elbertson was refusing to admit to himself the extent of his own weakness. He had been quite ill in the shower, had managed to slash himself rather badly with the razor while shaving, but was now smartly attired in a clean pair of the regulation tan shorts and T-shirt that was the equivalent of uniform aboard, with the insignia of his rank properly in place—and so weak he could hardly move.

The briefing had helped even less. The major knew himself guilty of negligence while on duty. Inadvertently, but as though by his very hand, certainly through the agency of some saboteur he had failed to spot, his weapon had been turned on his own troops at Thule, a key post in the plan.

It was possible that the entire plan had been sabotaged, though that seemed quite unlikely. Its ramifications were too great. So long as HOT ROD still existed, was still within their reach, the plan was operational.

The nonsense about a magneto-ionic effect he discarded without hesitation. Obviously it was sabotage, possibly by someone with a plan of his own, more probably by someone in the pay of one of the big power companies that would like to see the operation at least postponed. Nothing would be obvious until he knew in exact detail what had occurred, what the plans of the enemy would be, where next they would strike—and who the enemy was.

But that last, at least, was almost obvious. Who else, but the man who had carried the political battle, against all odds, that HOT ROD be created? Who else but Captain Naylor Andersen could possibly have delivered this sneaking, underhanded attack against himself and his comrades?

Who else, he thought, but a man so callous as to order *him*, sick as he was, to leave the bridge as though he were a mere cadet.

Steve Elbertson's mind was made up as to the identity of the enemy.

But he would have to proceed with care, or he would key the plan before the time was ripe. There must be no great shake-up in personnel, no undue attention from Earth to the potentials of HOT ROD. Perhaps the saboteur's cover story of a magneto-ionic effect would serve his ends as well—at least until his comrades on Earth signalled that the time was ripe.

Yet now that HOT ROD had proved its power, the time *was* ripe. It was that proof on which the plan had waited. And perhaps this very sabotage would prove more effective than the slower program originally planned . . .

Even as he fought to clear his normally organized mind of the weariness of his body that now sapped at its strength, the information he needed arrived.

Chauvenseer appeared at his side, saluting smartly. "Message from Com Officer Clark," he said, presenting his C.O. with a sealed envelope.

With almost-steady hands, Elbertson tore the envelope open.

"Operation Ripe Peach was initiated immediately after

the destruction of Thule, and is rephased to base its time-schedule on that overt action by the mad scientists. Earth orders that you take command of the satellite complex immediately. When your prisoners are secure and HOT ROD in operational condition, contact headquarters for further instructions." The message was unsigned.

Major Elbertson pulled himself to a military stance. Briefly he considered gathering all his men, all the Security personnel, and storming the bridge.

No. Obviously the enemy was organized—an unforeseen circumstance. Obviously the captain was not alone. Obviously the captain's men included at least some of the slipstick boys—and he had the added advantage that he would undoubtedly be able to command the loyalty of all the scientists, since he was somewhat of their ilk himself. No, an officer must seek the most advantageous position from which to deliver his ultimatum.

He must use HOT ROD itself to control them. If it were actually sabotaged . . . but no, that would not have been done. They would have needed HOT ROD themselves. They had undoubtedly cut off the power supply to the big laser, but that possibility had been foreseen.

HOT ROD, he decided, must be the first objective; the bridge the second.

"How much do those aboard know of what is happening on Earth?" he asked his aide.

"We haven't been able to contact Earth at all, sir, except through the official channels on Com Officer Clark's console. The flare drowned out all radio. I imagine they're rather upset, on Earth. They've kept the captain hunting for the saboteur who——"

"Our men?" snapped Elbertson.

"Our men have been on watch for the saboteur

146

too, sir. The captain stationed them outside each lab——"

"I mean, how much do our men know?"

"About what, sir?"

"About what's happening on Earth?"

"They know that Earth suspects sabotage, sir. They. . . ."

Elbertson smiled grimly to himself. That was just as well. He, and obviously Lieutenant Clark—theoretically civilian Com Officer Clark—were evidently the only two aboard who knew the true situation. If the captain, too, had been unable to contact Earth? . . . yes, he must be ignorant of what was going on, or he would surely have taken measures to protect himself while the commanding officer of Security forces aboard was still unconscious.

Earth Security must have been doing a tremendous job of bluffing, to have kept the lab personnel quiescent all this time; but they had done that job, and he must not spoil that advantage at the last moment.

He snapped, to Chauvenseer, "This is the detail of our immediate operation. Pass the word among our men to be exceptionally alert; to attach the single ear phone to their personal radios, and to remain tuned to our emergency frequency, Security Band 2Z21. They will receive their orders over that band.

"Now—they are stationed singly outside the bulkhead of each laboratory?" His aide nodded. "Have each man move inside the laboratory concerned. However, have them make no overt move other than to prevent anyone on board from taking any action that might be . . . that of a saboteur. Every civilian aboard is suspect, and any action that might possibly result in sabotage—anything unusual—is to be prevented.

"As for the bridge—how many men are stationed outside the bridge?"

"There are two, sir. In the central axial tunnel. One at each end, guarding the passenger entrances to the rim."

"That leaves how many?"

"Myself and four others, sir. The special four you reserved to your personal orders."

"Hmmm. Well, two should be sufficient at the bridge. Clark's there. And I'll need you and my four with me. Very well. Alert the men to their orders, then you and the other four proceed, as unobtrusively as possible, to the south polar lock. I will meet you there, and I will bring Smith with me.

"Execute!" he ended, saluting smartly.

On the bridge, Nails Andersen was deciding that Elbertson would probably snap out of it as soon as he had had coffee and a shave. The man had probably been severely affected by the radiation and the countering drugs, as well as by the sedation he had been given. It should not be necessary even to make a note of the temporary irrationality in the log, or to refer again to that erratic behaviour, unless it continued.

Having made the decision, he began making notes on just what details of the past few hours *would* go in the log.

Bessie, her carefully laid plans long since taped and coded for action, found herself suppressing the urge to improve on what she'd done. Comes the time to shoot the artist, she decided, before he does too much and ruins the painting.

There wasn't anyone to whom she could show the picture, who could say for her enough, but her own innate senses were satisfied. I've got the hands-off signal from myself, and I'd better obey it, she thought. The Cow is programmed and ready if—oh, wishfully not!—the drastic is necessary.

Putting a stack of paperwork in place, she began idly casting horoscopes while pretending to be busy. Most of the people on board knew of Bessie's "eccentricity," and it was one of the best disguises she had developed, as well as a study in action and reaction as people laughed at horoscopes and were subtly influenced by their predictions.

Odd, she thought, following the standard prediction operations she wasn't coming up with quite the innocuous results she expected. The houses of the various signs were continuing their heavy oppositions long after the unbalance shifted, and were giving negative readings across all the charts.

Chad Clark, having alerted Earth that the C.O. was conscious, back on duty, and had received a briefing and their orders, watched the other two on the bridge through his tiny mirror. Fiddling while Rome burns, he thought, as the captain pulled out the log.

On the rim, things were getting back to normal. The labs were functioning again, most of them according to their routine procedures. In some, heads were drawn together over the absorbing diagrams supplied by Mike and Ishie.

In the astronomer's quarters on the rim, Perk was fuming. He had been attempting to get a line through to Earth to consult with observatories there on some of the data received by his instruments during the flare. But, he'd been told, flare conditions had knocked out all but one line, and that was being reserved for official use. He considered putting a request for five minutes' use of the line through the captain, decided against it, and finally began the work of correlating the data received with his assistant, so they'd be ready with what conclusions they could draw when conditions returned to normal and the communications system was again open to use by the scientists.

It would be hours before the M.R. was down enough so that he could safely work in the observatory. The Security guard outside his quarters made him nervous; and though he assured both himself and Jerry that the inconveniences were quite understandable, he admitted that their combined irritation potential was high.

In the FARM, Dr. Millie Williams sat for a while in deep thought, very conscious of the guard who stood outside the bulkhead in her area, as well as the fact that there was a similar guard outside each of the other laboratories.

Finally, with a gesture of decision, she stood up, went to the intercom and ordered two lunches prepared by the cafeteria, then walked self-consciously past the self-consciously posed guards along the hallways to pick up the trays.

In the machine shop, Mike and Ishie were hard at work in one corner, while on the other side of the shop, Paul sang happily as he and Tombu wound coils.

There was a cough at the entrance to the machine shop, and Millie's soft voice said "May I come in?"

All four looked up as the slender figure of the dark-skinned biologist entered the lab, balancing two trays with carafes atop. She approached Mike and Ishie.

"If I know you, Dr. Ishie, and you too, Mike—you haven't eaten," she said with a smile. "Now have you?"

"Millie," said Mike, "you've just reminded me that I'm as hollow as a deserted bee-stump after the bears get through with it."

"Little Millie," said Ishie, looking up at the figure nearly as tiny as his own, "you must be telepathic as well as beautiful. Confusion say, 'Gee, I'm hungry.'"

"I'm told that the fate of the satellite depends on you two." Millie smiled. "I thought I'd just give our fate a little extra boost. Now drop what you're doing and light into this.

"After that, if you've got a job for a mere biologist, I've got my lab readied to where it can last till I get back—and I'm not bad with a soldering iron. Meantime, why don't you let Paul and Tombu go eat while you eat?"

"Good idea," said Mike. "You two. You heard the lady. We gotta give our fate the benefit of victuals. Scat."

As soon as the physicist and the engineer were settled to the containers of food and coffee she had brought, wolfing them down hungrily, Millie opened up.

"While we're alone," she said softly so that she could not be heard through the bulkhead. "I'm going to speak my piece. You two will do me the honor of not taking offense if I say that you have the most brains and the least consciences aboard—and I happen to share the latter characteristic."

The two looked up guiltily and waited.

"Now don't stop eating, for I'm not through talking," she said. "That magneto-ionic effect canceller that you dreamed up would probably cancel the six hundred forty pound magneto-ionic effect thrust you dreamed up—if such a thing existed.

"What I want to know—don't stop eating until you've decided whether you're going to let me in on your game or not—is what really does exist? I might be of some help, you know."

"But . . ." Mike and Ishie simultaneously choked over their food, looked at each other, then Mike blurted out, "But how could *she* know?"

"Quiet," said Millie. "Keep your voices down. The Security guards are stationed all over looking for a saboteur, and they might just decide that you're it.

"But don't worry about anybody else jumping to my conclusions. I'm probably the only one. It takes a person with little conscience and much imagination . . . takes a thief to catch a thief, I mean. Yes, I think I mean that quite literally. Besides, I can help with some of that glassware that disappeared out of my supplies several days ago. Oh yes, I knew it was gone and I knew where it went—but I figured any purpose you had in mind was a good one, Ishie.

"But for how I personally cancelled the idea of your magneto-ionic effect from the flare—it just happens that last night I was curious while everybody was asleep. When Bessie first came on duty this morning, I offered to relieve her while she had a cup of coffee, and I got a half-hour all by myself with the Cow. The captain wasn't up yet, and Clark was very busy talking to somebody over the communications board.

"The Cow's console is so simple that practically anyone with a basic knowledge of computers and cybernetics could figure out the mechanics of asking her questions.

"The first question I asked—something about our orbit—the Cow told me the information was top secret, and to get it I must go to the channel in the engineer's quarters and identify myself as Mike. I started to intercom you, Mike, to tell you that your machinations were showing, but Bessie came back about then.

"I hung around to see what would happen, and pretty soon Bessie asked the Cow the same question—but instead of getting the same answer, the Cow told her that an external magneto-ionic effect was pulling us out of line.

"So I went up to your engineering place, Mike. I rather thought you'd like to know what the Cow had told me —but Dr. Ishie was there, and so instead I went about my business until I could figure things out.

"Now I couldn't figure things out. But I could figure there's a monkey wrench somewhere—and since the two of you have been sticking together like Siamese twins, I know it will be perfectly all right to ask you in front of Ishie.

"Now," she finsished, "Do I get my girlish curiosity satisfied? You don't have to tell me. I'll just keep on being puzzled quietly and without indicating the slightest magneto-ionic dubiousness, if you'd rather. But I might be helpful; and I *would* like to know."

And she sat back quietly, while the two stared at her.

"Confusion say," Ishie finally declared through the side of his mouth, "that he who inadvertently put big foot in mouth is apt to get teeth kicked loose. We are very lucky, Mike, that it was Millie who asked the question of the Cow at that time. Besides, we've got to tell somebody sooner or later. We can't just run off with the wheel by ourselves.

"Yes, Millie," he added, "I think you have a job. Your help here will be appreciated of course. But what we really need is a way of bridging the gap between ourselves and the rest of the personnel before it gets too wide. How's your P.R. these days?"

"Public relations is something I learned in a very rough school," she answered nonchalantly. "Desegregation was at its full, flaming best when I was a girl back in Mississippi. But maybe I'd better know what the gap is."

The two began to talk, Millie shushing their voices

quieter as they interrupted each other, stumbled over concepts in their excitement, and incoherently outlined the Confusor and the various forces it exerted through what Mike kept calling its "inertial fishhook."

Finally, Mike took over, his voice low but intense with pleasure. "To put it simply," he said, "our pet didn't do at all what we expected. It hooked in on inertia and it took us off. A confusing little Confusor—but Millie it's a space drive. A real, honest-to-gosh *space drive.*"

Millie gulped. It was far, far more than she had expected. Perhaps this was another form of disguise like the magneto-ionic . . . ?

"Are you sure?" Then she answered her own doubts, sotto voce. "Of course you're telling the truth now. That's not something you two would play games about." Then in awe, "You've really got it?"

"Mosquito-sized. But real," Ishie confirmed.

"But why, then," she said, uncomprehending, "are you hiding it?" But before they could answer, she answered her own question again. "You'd have to. Of course. Otherwise it will be strangled in red tape. Otherwise nobody'll let you work on it any more, except as head of a research team stuck off somewhere. It would be declared top secret and you'd be treasonous if you even mentioned it. Otherwise, Budget Control would take it over and make a fifteen-year project out of it—and the two of you will probably have it in practical operation. . . ."

She looked at the molds and wiring taking form all over the machine shop.

"Oh no! You'll have it in operation soon!"

"Yes, soon—and we hope soon enough." Ishie sighed, then grinned impudently. "There is," he said, "the little matter of the fact that—in all innocence, but nevertheless quite thoroughly—we wiped out Thule Base.

"If we don't get the big Confuser in operation very soon, it may be that we shall spend a good deal of time in Earth's courts proving our innocence while someone else botches most thoroughly the job of creating a Confusor that could take us to the stars. And that," he added mournfully, "neither of us would enjoy. We might not even be able to prove our innocence, for there would be many people very anxious to prove us sufficiently guilty to keep us out of the way for many years.

"So you see," he said, "you have a very real P.R. problem. Our assistants here could work better if they knew what they were doing. The people aboard the wheel would be most excited by a space drive, and would give us every aid.

"But what the law says, it says—and the captain would have no choice but to put us in irons if he heard, though I think our captain is such that he would not want to do it.

"We must tell everyone what we have, for where the wheel takes us, they will go. But we can't tell them, for if we tell anyone, it will get back to Earth—and we murdered Thule, according to the law of Earth.

"It is a very neat problem," he said.

Major Steve Elbertson arrived at Project HOT ROD first, with the other six men trailing behind him on their scuttlebugs.

As he slipped through the lock and out of his spacesuit, he reached down the neck of his coveralls and carefully extracted the Security key in its flat, plastiskin packet, from between his shoulder blades. At least the villainous captain had not gotten his hands on this, he thought, and whatever damage had been done to HOT ROD probably could be quickly repaired.

Chauvenseer had told him of the hunt for the key, and he had been silently amused, though he had volunteered no information to his briefing officer.

Stepping forward as briskly as a sick rag doll, he fitted the key into the Security lock and snapped open the bar that prevented HOT ROD's use.

As the others entered, he turned to them. Supporting himself against the edge of the console and managing to look perfectly erect and capable despite his weakness, he said: "You were each advanced technicians in your former lives. I have instructed each of you to learn as much as you could of the operation of this device.

"It is now necessary that the civilian scientists," he pronounced the "civilian" as though it were a dirty word, "be relieved of their rule over this weapon, and that the military take its proper place, as masters of the situation.

"I trust each of you has learned his lessons carefully, because it is now too late for mistakes—although we have with us assistance far superior to that of the civilians.

"Gentlemen," he said, and his voice took on power as he talked, "it is a pleasure to reintroduce to you a companion whom you have known as Lathe Smith.

"This, gentlemen," he said formally, gesturing the civilian forward, "is the Herr Doktor Heinrich Schmidt, of whom you would have heard were you familiar with the more erudite developments of space physics.

"Dr. Schmidt," he added, "it is a pleasure to be able to again accord you openly the courtesies and respect that are your due.

"Now for myself," he continued, "it may surprise you to know that I, too, have a somewhat more advanced rank than you have suspected." Deliberately he unpinned the major's insignia that he wore, and brought out a sealed packet, opened it, and pinned on four stars.

"Gentlemen," he finished, "may I introduce myself? General Steven Elbertson, commanding officer of all space forces of the United Nations Security Forces.

"Now," he said briskly to his astounded men, his voice crackling with authority, "take stations.

"Dr. Schmidt will connect the storage supply that he has readied, which will activate the weapon.

"He will then key in the number one laser bank only. You will select as your target area that area through which the passenger spokes of the wheel pass. These will each in turn be your targets if it becomes necessary to fire.

"Dr. Schmidt has advised me that, should it become necessary to fire on the hub, the resultant explosion of the shielding water would wreck the entire wheel, which would not be fatal, but would leave us without a base from which to operate.

"However, if we should miss the spokes and hit the rim itself, the resultant explosion would inevitably wreck both the big wheel and Project HOT ROD. We ourselves should not survive such an explosion.

"Therefore, gentlemen, I caution the most accurate possible aim."

Quickly, then, he slid into the communication officer's seat, as the Security aides assumed each of the four major posts of the project, while Chauvenseer took up a stance at his general's right hand, ready to respond as directed.

XI

On the bridge, Nails Andersen felt his temper rising. The flood of messages, directives and counter-directives from Earth, showed no signs of abating even though the problem had been located and measures were underway to correct it. The search that was being demanded for a saboteur was taking on the proportions of a damned witchhunt. Earth was refusing to recognize the fact that no human agency *could* have given thrust to the wheel, except by puncture-jet, which had long since been shown to be nonexistent.

The paranoia—yes, Nails assured himself, paranoia was the proper term—on Earth was so great that there had even been one directive, and from a fairly high source, that had had the temerity to suggest that he give over command of the satellite to the "Security forces aboard, for the duration of the emergency. . . ."

Did the idiots behind that message think that command of the satellite was a political office whose personnel could be shifted in their patterns of authority at the slightest whim? A ship ran under a tight chain of command that could not be broached other than by formal, proven charges backed by orders from the head of the U.N. Council, and accompanied by appointment of a competent successor.

Nails was beginning to realize that he'd probably face a formal inquiry on Earth when he returned; but any competent board of inquiry would clear him immediately and without too many political repercussions.

Meantime, though, he'd have to make his bow to Earth in its witch-hunt demand for a saboteur by continuing the watch for the mythical 'enemy' and posting Security officers about. Their tan outfits with the various symbols of rank attached had seemed omnipresent before; now they were an overriding factor, creating a pall throughout the ship. Bad for morale, distasteful in the extreme, and a hampering influence on the work of rational men to

158

find the answer to the factors—the very real factors—
that confronted them.

He had not been blind to the political pressures by
which the laboratory's Security force had been maneuvered
into a controlling position aboard HOT ROD. The countermeasures that would return the big power beam to
civilian control were well prepared in bills to put the
beam to effective use in the service of Earth; bills that
would ride through Council on the heels of the upcoming
measures that would return the member nations much of
the power that their federation had usurped. Upcoming in
a matter of days now . . .

Nails' eyes narrowed. The destruction of Thule, if it
could be pinned on a saboteur—specifically on a citizen of
one of the Big Four nations—would go far towards killing
those bills, he thought. There were still vast numbers of
people who preferred the stagnation of a "Securitied"
world to the dangers and the advantages of competition;
preferring what was rapidly becoming a uniform, planet-
wide welfare-union, to the individualism and challenge
of rivalry. There were still those who feared the power of
the Big Four.

If Security could provide such a saboteur. . . .

*And I, myself, am the most likely candidate for such
a charge,* he realized suddenly. *I even messaged Earth myself that such sabotage could not take place without my
cooperation. If it could be proven that I have misused
HOT ROD. . . .* His eyes sought the panel that still
displayed the Hellmaker on its taut cable . . . and seven
figures riding the end of the cable to the air lock.

Elbertson, he thought furiously. And taking his men
out when the proton level is still too high to go beyond the
rim shielding. . . .

Then he stopped in mid-thought. This was no idle act of a man feeling the effects of drugs.

He dialed the intercom quickly to the HOT ROD crew's quarters on the rim. "Dr. Koblensky. Important," he said, keeping a tight control over his voice.

"Just a minute, sir," came the answer, and seconds that seemed like eternities passed before the scientist's calm voice answered, "Dr. Koblensky speaking."

"Have you sent a crew to HOT ROD?"

"Of course not, sir. The proton level——"

"Thank you." The captain switched off. As though with a physical jerk, the pattern of events fell into place in his mind. Security would take advantage of the accident at Thule to increase its hold over Earth; to kill the upcoming bills. And their first action must be to take control of the Hellmaker—and of the wheel.

The coil of anger in his stomach dissolved now, and the calm of action took its place.

It would take time to activate HOT ROD, and they would not take action until the weapon was activated. Then, they must take over the wheel. Once the wheel was theirs, and he himself probably dead, they could create whatever evidence they desired to back any charges they might have in mind; and the destruction of Thule would prove those charges.

Never mind that. They would attempt to take over the wheel, and their men were placed—as he, himself, had placed them!—in advantageous positions. The two guards in the axial hubway were probably posted to listen and report whatever he said. Whatever measures he took would be known. . . .

But would those guards know that Elbertson was on HOT ROD? Possibly not. So if he acted as though he were continuing the witchhunt, anything they overheard would appear normal.

He dialed the machine shop. "Dr. Ishie. Mr. Blackhawk. To the bridge, please. Immediately."

Now. How would they plan to use the laser?

While he planned, he made a final check. He dialed first Security quarters, then the hospital, asking for the major, leaving urgent messages that he report to the bridge when located, "to assist in a matter of the utmost importance."

Mike arrived first, breathless, Ishie right behind him.

"You needed——" Mike began.

"Mr. Blackhawk. The saboteur, several of them, are believed to be aboard HOT ROD." The captain's voice was crisp. "Can they activate it?"

"Captain, there's no saboteur. . . ." Mike was interrupted before he could finish the sentence.

"Gentlemen. I'm not asking you to be the judge of that. If the saboteurs are there, is there any way that they could activate HOT ROD?"

"Oh, they could have storage batteries aboard, I suppose." Mike didn't even pretend to be excited.

"Then we will assume they have, Mr. Blackhawk." The tone of the captain's voice told Mike he'd better darned well believe in those saboteurs or tell the captain the truth—and that quickly. "Now, assuming HOT ROD can be activated, we will also assume that their first aim will be to control the wheel. They would, therefore, aim at the hub and issue an ultimatum."

"They might aim at a target on Earth, and issue an ultimatum to us." Mike would play the game.

"No. We would refuse such an ultimatum. They would aim at us. Can you prevent that?"

Mike thought hard. He'd better come up with an answer to that one, saboteur or no.

"If they shot through the hub, they'd hit our shielding water and explode the hub-hull. That would wreck the wheel, and they'd need the wheel. The only place they could safely shoot us would be the passenger spokes, and that would take some pretty fine target shooting—with only one laser bank. They could do it though," he said thoughtfully.

"Assume, Mr. Blackhawk, that if they couldn't hit the passenger spokes, they'd be willing to destroy the wheel in order to gain control. Is there any way to prevent that?"

Mike stood completely silent for almost a minute. Then he grinned. "Sure," he said. "If we turned the rim towards HOT ROD, they couldn't fire into the rim without hitting the shielding there—and *that* would almost inevitably take HOT ROD with it. If we turn the lab so that only the rim is towards HOT ROD, it's suicide—not only for them, but for their prize—to shoot us."

"You will swing the rim of the wheel into that alignment as rapidly as it can possibly be done." The captain's voice practically lifted the two men off the bridge, and they were on their way to the engineering quarters with every appearance of the urgency they should have felt if they had not known who—or rather, what—was the real saboteur.

At the computer console, Bessie thought furiously. How many factors of the growing focus of events had she been missing during the flare? Quietly she instructed the Cow to use its telemetry channels to pick up resumes of Earth political events from Earth computer memory storage areas where the queries would not be intercepted by human monitors. She had forborne to use the channels casually, since eventually her use might be spotted; but events seemed to be building, and now the risk seemed warranted.

At the communications console, Chad Clark debated with himself. Should he call in the guards stationed now just outside the bulkhead, and take over? His orders were to wait until HOT ROD was activated, and he had no idea how long that would take. If he took over the bridge, and counteraction of some sort took it back—that could be quite serious. It would start things before his gang was ready, and could be quite the wrong thing to do.

The captain was still unaware, obviously, of Security's plans. His move was against "saboteurs." But if the wheel were precessed?

The precession could be reversed, Clark decided, once the bridge was theirs. It might be a quite fatal mistake to try to take the bridge prematurely.

Unobtrusively he slipped his needle gun from its hiding place and laid it on the console, hidden from the captain by his back, but within instant reach of his hand.

On their way through the morgue, Mike heard Ishie's soft voice behind him, slightly breathless. "At that, you'd better swing the rim and swing her fast, Mike. The captain sure 'nuff believes in his saboteurs, and it's just possible they're real."

Okay, thought Mike, and really moving now he reached the engineering quarters a good ten strides ahead of his companion.

As he entered the open bulkhead lock he saw a man in the tan shorts and shirt of one of the Security personnel, and brushing past him, said, "If you want to see me, come back later. I'm going to be very busy here for a while."

Mike headed for the panel that controlled the air jets and other devices that spun the wheel.

The Security guard didn't hesitate. Seeing the ship's engineer about to make important—and possibly subversive—adjustments, he drew his needle gun and aimed it squarely at Mike's back. "Halt! In the name of Security!" he barked.

Slowly Mike swung around, eyeing the man coldly, and began a question.

But there was no need. Ishie, having seen what was going on through the lock before he entered, had held back just long enough for the Security man to turn fully towards Mike. Now he launched himself through the lock like a small but well-guided missile, and arriving on the Security guard's back, had his gun-arm down and half broken before the man knew what was happening.

It was all that Mike needed. A karate chop to the neck finished the battle almost before it was begun. It hadn't been a clean chop in the light gravity, Mike decided, but obviously it had been sufficient. He took a few seconds to assure himself that the guard was indeed out of action, then turned back to the precession panel a bit more convinced that the captain had been right. No sabotage had caused the Thule disaster; but there were enemies aboard and they were showing their hand now.

The precession controls, though operational, had not to date been required. No haste now, thought Mike. Take it easy. Get it right.

Putting his mind completely on the task before him, he switched in the sequence that would put the controls into active condition, but not initiate their operation. That was left to the Cow.

Turning to the vocoder panel, and wording his command carefully, he directed the Cow to take over control of the now-active precession equipment; to use the sun as a referent for the axis of precession; and to move the pole ninety degrees in a clockwise direction around that axis of precession.

On the rim, valves between tanks began opening and closing. Water was switched north on one side of the wheel and south on the opposite side, the points of the switching always in a stable position relative to the spin of the wheel. Of the seventy-two valves spaced at intervals of five degrees around the rim, only two must be active at any time so that always the precessive force was aligned to produce the required motion.

The big wheel began to shift its alignment, slowly, precisely. The maneuver would take at least forty-five minutes, and the axis of the turn would be aligned directly on Sol by the computer. When it was finished, the rim of the wheel would be aligned, still with the sun, but also with Project HOT ROD, which had been to their south.

Assured that the precession was properly begun, Mike turned his attention back to the guard, and to Ishie.

That eminent physicist had left nothing to chance, he noted. The guard, already out, had been thoroughly trussed. While Mike watched, Ishie, for good measure, added two shots from the guard's own needle gun. A thorough workman, Mike thought admiringly.

Then Ishie looked up. "Let's store this—carrion—in the locker, Mike."

A good idea, Mike thought, and dragged the trussed body to the parts locker, moved a couple of shelves, shoved him in, and locked it.

Ishie was still breathing hard, but looking like a self-satisfied Siamese cat. "Confusion say those who play with firearms should be cautious," he said grinning. "Mike—we will precess?"

"Yes. It's started. But it will take about forty-five minutes. Maybe a little more."

"Well. It looks like somebody named Security is ready to play rough again, Mike. Is good to know they can't shoot us now—or at least in a little while, without getting themselves shot back. But they can shoot at Earth. Any ideas?"

"First we secure our own position here, Ishie. Lock the bulkheads to the morgue, will you? Locks are against regulations, and I hid them as best I could, but they're obvious if you're looking for them."

With that, Mike closed and carefully secured the other two bulkheads leading to the north pole of the hub; then jumped upward, grabbed the access ladder to the central axial tube, closed and bolted that one too.

Dropping back to the floor, he stepped over to the intercom and dialed the Captain's circuit.

"Mission accomplished, sir," he said. "And you were quite right. One of our *security servos* is off balance. We've attended to the matter."

"Thank you, Mr. Blackhawk." The captain's voice was calm, quite unlike the voice he'd used to them on the bridge. Then, "You would do well to listen for the . . . sound . . . of those servos." The captain's voice stopped, but the intercom continued to hum, alive, from his end.

"Oh, oh," said Mike. "The captain's already in trouble, and he's asking us to listen in on what goes on on the bridge. He's left the intercom open."

The hum continued, uninterrupted. The bridge was silent.

"Now I've got another mission to accomplish," continued Mike, "and you can't leave here, because this post's got to be operational. Keep the needle gun, and don't let anyone in, not even the captain. But anything you can do from here that the captain tells you over the intercom ought to be safe enough. So keep listening."

With that, Mike leaned over, loosened an inspection plate in the floor, and climbed down a ladder through the inspection tube that led at an angle through the six feet of normal-shield water around the hub, into the seventeen foot flare-shielding chamber beyond. This was the tank which surrounded the hub and held all the waters of the rim during flare conditions; but was now holding only the pressurized air supply which, during a flare, was pumped to the rim.

Making his way towards the center of the hub, Mike considered his luck in being one of the people most familiar with the entire structure of the ship. It would be unlikely that enemies operating aboard would think to cut off the air and water passages, or even keep them under surveillance. Nevertheless, he would be cautious.

He must now get to the machine shop and enter it without triggering any more of those—he laughed quietly to himself—security servos.

The particular tank he was in he had selected carefully. Of the twenty-one possible combinations, this one, he knew, would bring him into the water under the north hall that circled the outer rim.

In a few strides he reached the three-foot-diameter spoke tube through which the flood of water poured during a draw-in action such as they had had during the flare. He let himself over the side head first, let go and began falling down the seventy-nine foot length of the tube, accelerated by the light pseudo-gravity of the spin. Even so, he spread his legs and arms against the walls of the tube to act as brakes, so as not to arrive with too much impact at the bottom of the tube.

He hit the curve where the tube swerved around the

circumference of the rim to the point at its far side at which it entered its particular river, and his dive carried him to the bottom of the curve. Then he crawled up its far side to where the tunnel entered the rim river. There the motion of the fluorescent lighted water caught him, and he was swirled quickly to his target twenty-five feet along, Inspection Plate B-36. He grabbed the handhold by the plate before he was carried past, loosened the plate, lifted it only enough to be sure that the room was empty, and then pushed it off, pulled himself through, and emerged into the whining dimness of Compressor Room 9, next to the machine shop. The low whine assaulting his ears was that of the air compressors that fed the jets that drove the waters through the rim.

Stepping over to a wall locker, Mike took out a dry pair of shorts, a T-shirt and moccasins, kept there for the purpose of making changes after such swimming inspections of the rim tanks.

Then he stepped briskly into the corridor, glancing quickly both ways. It was empty. Quietly he moved to a position opposite the bulkhead to the machine shop.

To the right of the entrance, too far for surprise action, stood a Security guard, while across the shop from him Paul and Tombu grimly worked on, with Millie watching them.

On the bridge, Nails Andersen wasted no time in chastising himself for not being armed.

His first act was to write a note to Bessie. "We are under attack. Key the computer in such a way that it will take orders only if given the code-signal . . ." He paused. What was a code that each could remember under duress, but that would not be easily guessed? ". . . the code signal 'thulishness.' Then take a position by the bulkhead to the morgue, ready to secure it at my signal. Make no sudden moves. Act as though casually occupied. At my signal, close and bar that bulkhead."

As he finished the note, Mike's voice came over the intercom. "Mission accomplished, sir. And you were quite right. One 'of our *security servos* is off balance. We've attended to the matter."

The captain felt a surge of relief. Mike and Ishie were —at least partly—aware of the problem. Was there any way he could tell them what action to take? And if so, what action would he direct? There was no way, anyhow, but he could. . . . "Thank you, Mr. Blackhawk," he said, forcing calm into his voice. "You would do well," he would use Mike's own code, "to listen for the *sound* of those servos." Then he left his intercom open. At least they could keep track of what happened on the bridge, and act accordingly.

Now one more thing. He needed to get in touch with Earth, and he needed to block the bulkhead to the central axis tube.

Carefully he printed out a note to Clark: "We are under attack from Security itself. You will station yourself at the top of the ladder to the central axis tube, ready to secure the bulkhead there on my signal. Make no move that would alert the guards in the tube until you receive that signal, unless they start to come in. But be ready for instant action. We must not move until the wheel is precessed. I will take over the communications console and alert Earth to our situation."

Then he stood up casually and walked over to Bessie, laid the note on her console, and waited until she had read it.

She looked up at him startled. Was it time to key in her own code word? No, such drastic action should only be taken if there were danger of a takeover of Earth itself. She nodded at the captain and activated the Cow's teletype.

Satisfied that she understood and would carry out his orders, Nails moved, still casually, to the communications console.

As the captain approached, Clark slid the needle gun from before him into his hand. His hand went to his knees under the console.

He read the captain's note through, suppressing a grin; then nodded and slid from his seat, gun-hand out of sight behind his thigh. Keeping the gun shielded by his body from the other two on the bridge, he climbed the ladder to the axis-tube bulkhead, hooked one leg over a rung, and glanced down.

The captain had seated himself at the communications console, plugged in a channel, and was talking rapidly. Bessie had moved casually to a post beside the morgue bulkhead.

Okay, he thought. That's what Bessie's note told her to do. Good enough. We don't need that bulkhead anyhow; and she's just a girl. As for the captain, every channel is covered by our own men. Wonder if he'll find that out, or if they can keep him fooled a bit longer?

Mike entered the machine shop casually, as though intent on business. He brushed past the Security guard, and stepped over to the tape-controlled laser-activated milling machine as though to inspect its progress.

Then, as if finding an error, he halted its operation and swung the laser-head back away from the work-piece. The head swung free in his hand, attached to the machine but nevertheless free. Casually, without even looking at the guard, he centered the laser directly on him. Just as casually, he stepped to one side.

"The beam from this machine is quite capable of milling the hardest materials," he said, as though to himself. "Even a diamond can't withstand it." Now he looked directly at the Security guard. "It's capable," he said in an even tone, "of milling a hole right through your guts if you even so much as breathe too deep."

He told Paul: "Move around behind him, out of range of this beam, and secure the man, please. Millie, is there anything in your department that will make sure he won't talk for a while?"

"Yes, Mike, but I don't think I'd better go there right now. There aren't many of them, but these boys seem to be spread out all over."

Paul had the gun now, and the personnel communicator from the Security guard as well. He'd unhooked the unobtrusive ear plug from the man's ear, and that dangled.

"Okay," said Mike. "I don't think he can give us much trouble in there." He pointed to the air-lock bulkhead through which he had just entered. "Tie him well, and shut him in from both sides. We can go in and out through the physics lab," he said. "Best we shut that off now before some more of these boys wander along."

When both the lab and the Security guard were under control, Paul turned to Mike. "That milling-laser," he said. "It's got a focus of about six inches maximum. How did you fix it so it could burn the guard at that distance?"

"I didn't," said Mike briefly. "He already knows that lasers can reach from here to Earth. Why should I bother to lecture him on the differences in focal ranges?" Turning to Tombu he handed him the Security man's radio.

"See if you can rig this," he said, "to broadcast everything they say over the general intercom channel. It's about time we let people know what's happening."

It took Tombu only minutes to hook in the radio. As he turned it on, Elbertson's voice came over the loudspeaker system. A roll call of Security men was apparently being completed. The last three men responded as called.

Then Elbertson's voice, crisp though somewhat labored, came over the Security beam, booming throughout the ship.

"It is obvious that the renegade scientist Chi and the engineer of the wheel have replaced the men guarding their sectors.

"As we were informed, the captain has put them in charge. Since they struck the first blow, it is now up to Security to converge on them and eliminate them.

"Jones, Nickolai and Stanziale are detailed to the Dr. Chi mission. Nilson, Bernard and Cossairt are detailed to get the Indian. The rest of you will take over where you are posted, and secure all personnel to their quarters.

"Clark. Drop your cover and take over control of the bridge. The two men in the axis tube will join you and back you up.

"I expect to have HOT ROD operational within five minutes. And Clark, instruct the computer to discontinue precession operations that have been initiated.

"Take whatever measures are necessary to carry out these instructions.

"This is no longer an undercover operation, gentlemen. Security is taking control."

XII

On the bridge, the captain was outlining the situation on the wheel as rapidly as possible to the highest authority he had been able to reach. He had asked that his message be taped and gotten to the U.N. Council president on top priority urgency rush.

His sentences were succinct as he explained . . . and then stopped in mid-sentence.

Elbertson's voice was coming over the intercom, counting down his personnel, issuing instructions. . . .

"That is Major Elbertson's voice you hear," he said over the phone. "I will leave this channel open. Tape everything that occurs here." Hastily he keyed the channel into a microphone installed for broadcast periods that would pick up anything on the bridge.

Over the intercom Elbertson's voice was saying, "Clark, drop your cover and take over control of the bridge. . . ."

The captain looked up at Clark to see a needle gun pointed directly at him.

Inwardly, the captain groaned. Hopelessly, helplessly, he realized that this was not a new-born scheme. Nor confined to the Wheel. Who else, he wondered. . . .

He glanced at Bessie. She had started to secure the bulkhead, seen Clark's action, and stopped, staring at him open-mouthed.

Slowly, Clark came down the ladder, followed by the two guards from the axis tube. The three needle guns were unwavering.

"Tie him up, boys," Clark said to the guards. Then to Bessie: "Stop the precession of the wheel."

As she moved, stiffly, towards the computer console,

he changed his order. "Never mind," he said. "I'll take care of the Cow myself." And to the guards, "Secure this one, too."

Waiting until the two guards had the captain partially trussed, the girl seated and her hands tied, Clark moved to the computer console and activated the teletype.

"The precession you have initiated is to be reversed immediately," he typed out. "Return the wheel to the position it had before the precession was started."

The screens above the console flickered. A display of HOT ROD that had remained constant since the flare blanked out, and all thirty-six screens came alive with electronic patterns that danced in disconcerting snowfalls and iridescent displays.

The Cow's teletype activated and chattered out, "The wildlife of Earth falls roughly into the classes of vertebrates. . . ."

"Stop," Clark typed in as an order. But the dissertation on the varieties of Earth wildlife continued. He switched off the teletype, waited a moment, switched it on again. The inconsequential irrelevancies continued as soon as the teletype was switched on.

"Any prior orders to this one will be disregarded, and you will now. . . ."

The chatter of the teletype continued as the Cow produced data on wildlife that seemed destined to keep up as long as the teletype was electronically capable of pursuing the subject.

Clark looked disgustedly at the facts and figures being spewed forth onto the tape, then looked at the captain.

"So you managed to put the Cow out of control? Okay," he said. "I think we can handle this." Then to the guards: "Untie the girl."

Untied, Bessie sat still, staring at her former colleague.

"All right," he said in a cold voice, "You can't hold out. So you might as well give in before things get real grisly. The Captain could not have discombobulated the computer himself, not at any time since the flare, because I have been on the bridge every minute of that time, and he has not been at your console. Therefore, you are the one who did it, and you will know how to undo your actions.

"You will now take the Cow out of this blithering idiocy and have it return the wheel to its former position, or you will watch while we slowly, but quite surely, butcher your beloved captain. Do you believe me, or shall I demonstrate?"

"Bessie! Don't. . . ." The captain was silenced by a blow across the mouth, and Clark spoke to him softly.

"Heroics would be quite unjustified here, Captain. You have already lost, whether you cause us to take the time to butcher you, or simply let matters take their course. Whether you are executed painfully here, or quite humanely on Earth is up to Bessie. But executed you will be, as I shall show you." He turned to the communications console radio receiver and activated it, switching its broadcast from his own earphones to the ship's loudspeaker. "We will also allow all ship's personnel to realize that they are helpless," he said as he switched stations until he got a news summary that was replaying the original "newscast" from the "mad scientists."

Slowly the fantastic pattern of retold events pieced itself together in a picture in Nails Andersen's mind—a picture that came through with almost the force of a physical blow as he heard the "mad scientists'" demands —*in his own voice,* while the screen showed him on the bridge, shaking his fist at the mike. *His own voice*—demanding, demeaning Earth, abrogating to his ship and his people the right to control Earth, to be supported by Earth in a vast program. . . . and the pictures of the scientific personnel of the ship clapping and cheering. . . .

Nausea threatened to swamp him. His ears registered the chuckles and gloating phrases with which Clark was underlining each bit of the pattern as it dropped into place as part of a whole picture, but those comments remained peripheral.

His own voice. . . .

The radio was switched off, and Clark was standing over him. "You can see, Captain," the man's voice was saying, "that it is only a question of where and in what manner you shall be executed."

Clark turned then to the girl. Her face was white. She looked once at the Captain, helpless on the floor against the bulkhead, then at him. "Do you believe now," he asked, "that I shall use any method necessary without compunction to get your . . . cooperation?"

"I'm . . . I'm afraid I believe you, Chad," she said. "I . . . I wish I didn't. I. . . ." She began to sob bitterly, unable to speak through her sobs.

Clark opened her private drawer in the console and pulled out a finger nail file. He turned it over carefully in his fingers. "A rather blunt instrument," he said calmly, "but it should do until we can send for better." He approached the captain.

"No!" Bessie screamed. "I could hold out for a bit, Captain," she said through her sobs.

"Hold out, Bessie!" The captain was silenced again with a blow, and this time his mouth was stuffed with a T-shirt, tied in place with a belt.

"No," she said, "I could hold out for a bit, but not for long. I'll . . . I'll tell them now, before. . . ." She swallowed hard. Then: "The code word is, first, *Boojum*," she said. "After that, you key in the word *Thulishness* and the Cow will obey any order." And again, sobs wracked her body.

On board HOT ROD, the Security crew was working against an accelerated time-schedule now. The storage batteries that would provide a power supply had been wired into the big weapon—an exacting operation requiring both skill and time. Now the interminable countdown was underway as each component was brought alive and checked in correct operating sequence. Then the factors could be keyed in that would bring the mirror in an arc, turning it to bear precisely on that area of space through which the passenger spokes of the wheel turned. But the aiming controls of HOT ROD's big mirror too were infinitely precise—and correspondingly slow.

As the crew of HOT ROD strove to get it into position to fire; and the computer on the wheel strove to precess the wheel to a position where firing would be fatal to the firer, it became a race between giant snails.

It was a curious sensation, seeing the big wheel from this angle, Chauvenseer caught himself thinking. Much the sensation of an ant, staring at the oncoming wheel of a huge truck.

In the machine shop, Mike was rummaging around in one of the tool lockers. "Any sort of a small telescope," he muttered almost to himself. Then, "Paul, is there a theodolite or anything like that left lying around in here?"

"Yes," said Paul, moving off to a cabinet in another part of the room. "We needed them when we were putting the wheel together."

"Okay." Mike turned back to the laser milling machine. "Now can we take the focusing lens off of this, and rig something to give me a focus at about four and a half miles? Or would it need focusing at all? Shooting at that distance?"

"Depends on what you shoot, Mike. The unfocused beam can make a black surface very hot very quick. But from a mirror surface, it would just bounce, unless it's carefully focused."

"It ought to take care of the plastic at least, then."

"Go right through it. You gonna laser the Hellmaker?"

"Not exactly. Here, make me a bracket to fit these two things together, so I can see what I'm aiming at." He handed the theodolite telescope and the laser milling-head to Paul.

"How much of the machine do I have to take to power that milling-head?" he asked Tombu.

"Not much. Most of it's just control circuits. This box on the back is the power supply. Plugs right in to the ship's power."

"Hey!" Mike called over to Paul now busy constructing a bracket. "Make that bracket to hold this power supply too. Oh, and round me up about sixty feet of extension cord, Tombu."

"But, Mike, how are you going to get out there?" Millie's voice was concerned. "They've probably got men all over the place out here on the rim. If you try to go through the corridor towards an emergency lock, they'll have you sure with their needle guns. You heard Elbertson delegate three men to kill you."

"I expect I can find a place where they aren't." Mike patted her briefly on the arm, then picking up the Security radio from the intercom bench, he turned it on and spoke into it, his voice going out over the intercom as well.

"Elbertson. This is Mike Blackhawk. You now have twenty minutes to surrender." And he cut off.

Mike turned to Tombu. "Get me some plastic wrapping material. Preferably a plastic bag. I've got to make this stuff waterproof."

When the power supply, telescope, milling head and extension cord were rigged and carefully wrapped in plastic to make a waterproof package, he attached them with a shoulder rope.

"Too bad we didn't make a lock in the wall right here," he muttered. "But I don't suppose Security will be guarding those empty labs over in the R-12 sector. Guess I'm going for a swim now." And with that, Mike reached down and carefully removed the inspection plate from one of the floor tanks, and lowered himself over the edge into the racing waters.

Hanging there with one hand, he carefully pulled the plastic bag into position beside and slightly behind his body, and let go. Instantly he was sucked away into the subdued blue fluorescent glow of the waters of the rim.

Glad they figured these planktons need light, he thought to himself. I'd have a time finding where I'm going in the dark.

Forty-five seconds later he reached up and snatched at a passing hand-hold next to a plate marked with the numbers of the lab he sought.

Wrenching the handle of the inspection plate and pushing it free, Mike climbed out into the deserted lab. He made his way out into the corridor, his unwieldy package hanging to his shoulder and runlets of water making a trail behind him—and stepped into the nearby emergency lock.

In the lock he quickly donned one of the emergency spacesuits that hung there, gathered up his bundle again, and stepped out on the catwalk of the inner part of the rim, under the brilliant night sky at the moment, but turning towards its "sunrise."

He attached his safety line to a nearby guideline, part of the rim's "hairnet," then opened his plastic package and fitted the end of the extension cord into a plug beside the lock which used carbon brushes to make contact so as to prevent vacuum welding. Then he turned on the Security radio.

"Major Elbertson," he said. "You now have five minutes to surrender."

He crept over the inside edge of the rim. From this position he had a full view of the glowing bubble that was HOT ROD, and of the mirror that was inching its bulbous-nosed way towards a focus, for the few seconds until the movement of the rim took him past the "sunrise" point and turned him sunwards.

Last time Mike had been outside on the rim, the wheel had not been turning. There'd been no reference of up and down. Now he felt disoriented. The wheel was spinning, the hub therefore seemed "up." And from the edge of the rim where he clung to its hairnet, all directions were down. The push of centrifugal force was towards the stars that seemed to sweep beneath his feet and over his head, and though it was a slow pattern of movement —only twice as fast as the crawl of a second hand around the face of a clock—and a light push, he clung to the hairnet, and wedged himself tightly into it, with his back braced against the rim.

Firmly braced, he adjusted his bizarre "gun" to rest on his knees so that he could sight in the direction that was, to his body's senses, straight down. Not at all, he thought, like trying to shoot fish in a barrel. More like being the fish and trying to shoot the people outside the barrel.

Back in the shadow again. Not really shadow where he sat, but the rim around him, below him, and curving away from him, had disappeared in its brief nightside, and there came the Hellmaker again. Carefully he tracked it; then putting his eye to the scope he focused briefly on one of the high-pressure supporting tubes that formed the structure by which the aiming mirror was held in place.

And fired.

The tube burst noiselessly but quite spectacularly. And the mirror itself shuddered as the tube's gases escaped.

Now he was in bright sunlight again, quickly closing his eyes as the sun looked full into them and slowly passed, to be followed by Earth, to be followed by a blank stretch of starry space, and here again was HOT ROD.

Carefully he tracked another of the focusing mirror's supporting tubes.

And fired.

And again a spectacular, writhing collapse—and this time, the mirror fell free, supported by only two tubes and incapable of aiming the monster beam.

HOT ROD was secure from the misapplication of Security.

"Three minutes," he spoke into the radio. "Your weapon is dead. My next shot will be through the nitrogen tank at your air lock. I wouldn't advise you to be there."

The wheel turned once more, as the radio came alive from the other end.

"Mr. Blackhawk, do you realize that what you are doing constitutes mutiny in space and will be dealt with accordingly on Earth? I have officially taken control of HOT ROD at the command of my superiors in the U.N. Security Control Command."

Mike didn't bother to answer. As the wheel turned him towards HOT ROD again, he said into the radio, "Two minutes."

Elbertson's voice came again. "With this new weapon we control Earth. Don't you realize that you can't stand up against the new people's government of Earth?"

The wheel came around. Mike spoke again. "One minute."

The lock on the HOT ROD control room opened. Frantic tiny figures burst forth, activated scuttlebugs, and started on the five mile trek back towards the big wheel.

Paul and Tombu watched as Mike disappeared through the trap door in the floor into the swirling water beneath.

Then they looked at each other and grinned.

"Action stations," said Tombu softly, picking up the Security guard's gun. "Will you be okay here, Millie?"

"I have my own action station," she said noncommittally.

Paul scanned over the racks and shelves, glanced at a small torch, passed it by and settled on a high pressure grease gun which was both handily hefty and had the capability of squirting a spoonful of grease across an entire lab area. Not lethal, he decided, but definitely a gooey mess to get hit in the face with.

Without a word the two men turned to the corridor, peering out briefly to be sure it was empty, then making their way along it to the bulkhead beyond the already secured physics lab.

They poised before the bulkhead only briefly, then at a nod from Tombu, Paul thrust the door open, squirting his gun into the face of the guard inside and brushing past him, while Tombu needled the guard as he turned to aim at his first adversary. As the guard went down, a Bunsen burner cracked onto his skull as Dr. Carmencita Schorlemner joined the fray, wielding the only weapon she'd found available.

The chemistry lab was secure.

At the next bulkhead, Paul and Tombu used the same tactics bursting in, but stopped abruptly and grinned. Dr. Paul LaValle was rising from beside a prone guard, hypodermic in hand, while small animals of all types bounded around the lab making a confusion that was hard to keep track of.

"I just gave him a second shot," the scientist said, happily pushing the prone figure with his toe, and warding off a rabbit with an arm. His pudgy figure looked rather absurd, wielding the hypodermic aloft. "The shots weren't too large," he added. "I think the guard will recover. I let the animals out to give me an excuse to chase them, and I managed to get behind him with the sleepy gun I keep for loose animals."

Again a bulkhead, and again they used the one-two system for bursting through the door—and stopped as they entered.

Dr. P.E.R. Kimball was pouring liquid over the prone figure, and the fumes of ammonia were so thick that Paul's and Tombu's eyes were already beginning to water. Jerry held another bottle of ammonia waiting, tears pouring from his eyes.

"I went to the darkroom where we have lots of acid when I heard the order for the takeover," Perk explained in his clipped accents, swerving the guard's head around to cover all its area heedless of the tears dripping from his eyes. "I must neutralize the acid before it burns him too thoroughly. Then we can air the lab."

"But did the acid put him out?" Tombu asked respectfully.

"Oh, not at all," Perk replied with a thin smile. "It simply took his attention, and I kept dodging with it in front of him, until Jerry could come up from behind, get his gun and needle him."

Leaving the astronomers to their work, Paul and Tombu headed for the next laboratory. . . .

The entire rim was secure before the booming voice of the newscast keyed in from the bridge came over the intercom.

On the bridge, Clark smiled coldly as he returned to the console of the big computer. He typed in *Boojum* and the screens continued their inane flow of pictures and data, but in the electronic innards of the Cow circuits came alive; impulses found passageways; programs began to be fed with microsecond speed through her data channels to Earth, to the vast network of computers that webbed the Earth electronically, interconnected though not interdependent.

The interconnections came alive; instructions went out; computer programmed computer in a widening ripple that shortly encompassed a civilization—a network activated in microsecond pulses to pre-written programs that took minutes to key in, and that were followed by instant action.

Carefully, Clark typed in the world *Thulishness*. Without deviating by so much as a nanosecond from the program being coded to Earth, the Cow cleared her bridge screens and teletype channel and waited for orders.

"The precession you have initiated is to be reversed immediately," the order came. "Return the wheel to its original position."

While initiating precession reversal, the Cow switched

a few of its lesser circuits to a search of its memory banks for the coordinates of the position ordered. The search took almost a full second. Then she began the task of utilizing the mosquito thrust of the Confusor in her ship's interior in such a manner that it would eventually, after a large number of orbits, reach the spot the order specified.

Then, with one corner of her myriad attention, while the vast majority of the impulses flowing along her channels continued direction of the operation Earthside, she responded to the opening of the vocoder circuit from the engineering room where Ishie had been listening to the occurrences on the bridge.

"Give me a brief outline of the actions to be taken upon receipt of the code word *Boojum*," the voice asked.

While the microsecond pulses played through her data lines to Earth, the Cow placidly answered in the slow motion of the voice she had been given in the engineering quarters. "The code word *Boojum*," she said, "instructs me to initiate a program devised by Bessie a few days ago of combining the efforts of all Earth computers in patterns that will isolate and hinder actions leading to human dependence on a dictatorship there, while making possible any actions of individuals that lead to individual freedom for everyone."

"Whew," Ishie exclaimed. "*That Bessie. . . .*" Then, "The program called for by the code word Boojum is to be continued. Now, give me a brief outline of the actions to be taken upon receipt of the code word Thulishness from the bridge."

"This code word Thulishness activates me to clear my screens and to receive and act on orders from the bridge teletype circuit," the Cow replied.

"What orders have you received since that activation?" the voice asked.

"I have been ordered to reverse the precession of the wheel," the Cow mooingly responded, "and have initiated such action." There was a half-spoken word at the far end, but the Cow was continuing. "I have also been ordered to return the ship to her original position, and have determined that the coordinates of this location are. . . ."

The voice from the engineering compartment interrupted.

"The order to reverse the precession of the wheel is cancelled. Reactivate the order to precess .the wheel on which you were acting before the word Thulishness was keyed in. Cancel the order to return the wheel to its original position . . . and, Cow, what was the original position to which you were returning us?"

"The position in which the ship was located at the time of my activation," the Cow replied.

There was a small chuckle from the far end of the circuit, then:

"Any further orders from the bridge teletype circuit will not be acted upon until relayed to this circuit and confirmed from these engineering quarters," the voice told her. "Do you understand?"

"Yes," the Cow replied.

On Earth the programs the Cow was keying in were already taking effect. The true facts of what had happened aboard Space Lab I were being stored where they could be activated for printout in any number of odd contexts, and were being played on as many TV screens as could be computer-preempted for the purpose. It would be some hours before Security could bring this means of sabotage to its carefully laid plans under control.

Meantime "official" orders were going out on most normal computer-serviced channels that caused dismay and confusion at the receiving ends, but that could not be queried because of a mass of confusion in the communications channels that made any queries impossible.

Orders directed immediate release of all prisoners at each of the concentration camps; orders gave field commission rank to civilians that elevated them above the ranks of local commanding officers; orders transferred personnel on widely scattered missions that effectively disbursed them and frequently contributed to the sabotage. Other orders directed field units to proceed to the nearest prisons, storm them, and release all prisoners; to take prisoner political and corporate personages who had been formerly thought to be Security-minded and were now accused of betraying Security; orders to divert material from one spot to another; orders sending planes and ships to isolated areas.

Blackouts came and went across the planet as the vast networks of power grids responded to waves and sloughs of current as unpredictable as their source; communications were not simply fouled in many areas; it was shortly found that by picking up a telephone you could listen in to top Security conversations.

But perhaps the most permanently effective sabotage of the few days grace period before the computers could be taken over and placed under the control of their normal overlords, was in the banking system.

It was big money that was played with—no account under $5,000 was touched—but above that limit, on the local level, monies were transferred from account to account in a pyramiding system that left large amounts in the hands of selected persons. The selection was made from the computerized records to be found in most areas, in which almost any individual of a community is listed with a history whose detail would amaze most people; and they were selected on the basis of their history of control operations.

At national levels, monies were shifted from corporation to corporation and then to individual accounts; from governmental bureau to governmental bureau, and from there to individuals. And when it would be found, as it inevitably would be, that the sum of the shifting left credits of billions in the accounts of the individuals who headed Security and of the corporate cohorts with whom they were hand in glove, the hunt would be on, and would extend to the local scene, where the same pattern of pyramiding finances in the hands of local control artists would be uncovered.

The public reaction predictably would be violent, and would create as much disruption as the current program was causing.

The code word *Boojum* initiated a program that could last only days—but that was leaving behind it the seeds for volcanic disruption far into the future. Meantime, the chaos being created would take years to straighten out, and would give mankind the possibility of wresting freedom from his overlords before and while those overlords were recovering from the successive blows being struck.

On the rim, Mike worked his way back through the clinging net to the catwalk, failing completely to see the figure that dodged beneath the rim as he approached.

Glancing around, he carefully scanned over the entire inner rim before stepping out into the sunlight of the catwalk itself. Nothing.

Then a blink caught his eye, and he glanced towards the hub. There. In the observatory at its north end.

He thought for a minute that someone was signalling,

but finally decided that it was only a touch of sunlight on the shiny surface of the automatic tracking telescope which poked its nose out of the open shutters of the airless observatory, still doing its automatic job of recording solar phenomena in the absence of the astronomers.

Instead of re-entering the lock as he had intended, Mike linked his safety line to one of the service lines that lay along the nearest spoke, and kicked up it.

The safety snap dragged heavily on the line as Mike's partly-freed mass tried to fly off at a tangent. Surprised, and then berating himself for the goof, Mike grasped the safety line and went up hand over hand to the rim shield where he could swing himself into its net and make his way on to the open observatory.

Reaching the bulge at the end of the shielding tank, and crawling up over it, Mike made his way up at an odd, reversed angle through the netting and across the interface between the spinning hub and the stationary catwalk around the observatory. The change of velocity wasn't much but Mike found it a tricky maneuver. He climbed into the observatory dome through its open shutter.

Still in open vacuum and now in free fall conditions, Mike carefully checked the lock at the main axis to make sure that he could get into it without setting off an alarm. There was no sign of such an installation, and the lock showed vacant.

Just as he was about to enter it, he caught the shadow of a spacesuited hand clutching the edge of the open shutter through which he had entered.

Mike stepped into the lock, closed it behind him as though he had seen nothing, and cycled the lock. But he did not remove his suit, and he did not leave.

As the lock showed clear, the observatory bulkhead opened again, and two spacesuited figures confronted each other. Mike, laser gun raised, gestured the other into the lock, then switched on a light. Abruptly he lowered the laser.

"And just what are you doing here?" he asked as the air around them became sufficient to throw back his helmet.

"You might have needed help," answered Dr. Millie Williams in a small, scared voice as she shook out her long hair.

"And just *what*," Mike asked, "were you planning to do about it besides having me shoot you by mistake?"

Millie held up an oversize pair of dividers. "The Security people," she said, "are not the only ones with weapons. I borrowed this from the machine shop."

Mike stared down at the odd-looking, double-pointed "weapon."

"It's hard," Millie continued, "to look at more than one thing at a time through a space-suit helmet. I could've got 'em in the air hose while you held their attention."

Mike's chuckle was just a trifle ragged, and his mutter about bloodthirsty panthers didn't really go unheard as he began shucking his spacesuit.

This was the most dangerous point, Mike knew. The axis tube went from the observatory straight through to the south polar lock, with nothing to block sight or sound from travelling its length. They'd have to simply chance it. Their space suits off, he opened the lock.

Thier luck held. No Security guard was to be seen in the axis tube.

Four feet along the passageway, Mike stopped, used a special key to open an inspection plate, and they dropped lightly into the flare-shielding tank that now held only air. From there the pair back-tracked Mike's original path to the inspection plate in the engineering quarters, and so into his own bailiwick where they found Ishie standing catlike guard, a wrench in one hand, waiting for whatever might come.

"Confusion say," the grinning Chinese physicist declared, "two for one is good luck.

"But the captain is in bad circumstances, Mike," he added soberly. "And the ship is completely taken except for here. Bessie has fouled up their program on Earth a bit I think, but the shuttle is coming up with reinforcements for Lab I Security. Earth has decided that the Captain killed Thule Base and did it on purpose.

"And we are all charged," here his humor overcame his solemnity, "we are all charged, Mike, with mutiny on the high spaces."

But Mike was paying little attention. Striding diagonally across the circular floor, he reached for a bank of switches that were marked *Air Lock Cycling System,* and without hesitation flipped two of the switches to *off.*

The locks at the north and south polar hubs were now inoperable.

Then Mike moved to a panel marked *Spoke Damage Control,* and began flipping switches that would evacuate and render impassable the various spokes from the wheel to the hub.

"As my instructor in Confusion would say," Mike turned from the panel, "division is the better part of winning."

Then, as an afterthought, Mike walked over to a panel marked simply, *Scuttlebug Power,* and depressed that switch to *off.*

191

"I wonder," he said, "how good a monkey Major Elbertson is, when it comes to climbing a couple of miles of anchortube by hand."

XIII

On the bridge Bessie continued to sob, the sobs seeming to wrack her body. *I'm a damned good actress,* she thought. *They sound very real, and they must be extremely distracting.* Beneath the act her mind was racing. *Had the Cow had time to get its program through yet? Would the captain be able to get his bonds loose?* She knew he would be working at it.

His feet still looked very secured, but his hands were behind him and any motions would have to be very quiet not to attract attention.

Clark was hunched over the communications console his back to her, seemingly intent. The nail file with which he had threatened to butcher the captain lay on the edge of the console, quite out of her reach. The two guards were alert but, she felt, at least slightly sympathetic to the sobbing woman on the floor.

Over the intercom came Elbertson's voice. "Clark. Get somebody out to the south hub with a line. We've been de-powered out here on the anchor tube."

Clark turned briefly, and Bessie increased her sobs, slightly but irritatingly.

"Joe, get up to the hub and throw them a line. There's one in the air lock. And Franz. Shut that damned woman up."

As the one guard disappeared on his errand out the

hatch, and Clark turned back to the console, the second guard gestured at Bessie with his needle gun, but her sobs just became more uncontrollable. Clark half-turned in irritation, but turned back to his console, talking rapidly.

The guard started towards Bessie, his hand open to slap. At that instant the captain, still bound, made a violently convulsive movement, catching the guard's attention, and he turned in that direction.

It was all that Bessie needed.

Uncoiling from the floor like a taut steel spring, she struck the guard squarely in the back, tumbling him towards the captain and managing to push herself off again in a leap that carried her on towards the communications console.

As Clark began to turn she was on his back, her left arm around his face, pulling his head back; her right hand grasping the finger nail file. With all her strength she shoved the fingernail file into the exposed larynx, and ripped sidewise; then held him for seconds until he slumped, unconscious.

Meantime, as the guard was thrown towards him, Nails had only his knees to strike with, but he timed his motions so that as the guard came down his kneecaps were coming up, and caught the guard under the chin. It wasn't enough of a blow to put the guy out, but it threw him aside, and Nails rolled his bound body against him, struggling to get on top of him, wriggling and pounding with his head and knees.

That kept the guard out of action long enough. Bessie felt Clark sag, then flung herself back, and grabbed his gun where it had fallen on the center of the deck. She took careful aim and fired at the only exposed portion of the guard—his rump. It was seconds before the shot took effect from that location, and Bessie was standing over him until he sagged. But another shot proved unnecessary.

Then she scrambled monkey-like up the ladder and secured the hatch into the central axis tube, before untying the captain.

The captain paused only long enough to be sure that the guard was completely out and Clark thoroughly dead before going to the intercom he had left open.

"Mr. Blackhawk." His voice was ragged but formal. "The bridge is secure. Report on the engineering quarters."

"All secure in engineering, sir. Also, the guard sent to the hub is secured in the lock there—I turned on the cycling system so he could get in, then turned it off while he was inside so he couldn't get out. Major Elbertson and his gang are secured about a quarter mile out the anchor tube towards HOT ROD. The Hellmaker is inoperable. I have no reports from the rim, sir."

The captain keyed the machine shop on the rim.

"Machine shop? Is anyone free to answer?"

"Glad you called, sir," Tombu's booming voice answered happily. "We were just tooling up to storm the bridge, but I gather that's not necessary? The whole rim is secure, sir."

The captain paused only a moment, then keyed in the overall ship's intercom.

"Congratulations to each of you," he said. "The entire ship is secured. However, a shuttleload of Security forces is being readied for takeoff, and we have only a period of time that may be as much as three days.

"Each of you is now in charge of securing the guards you have overcome. As soon as thorough measures have been taken to secure . . ." he paused. "This is a word I find offensive," he said. "As soon as measures to make certain of their captivity have been taken, the entire personnel of the ship is asked to meet in the cafeteria."

"Captain?" Ishie's voice came over the engineering intercom. "Would you do me the honor of pasting me into the ship's intercom? There is a little thing I think everybody should know so they can be thinking while they captivate Security, sir."

"Dr. Chi. It is our honor. You are now on ship's intercom, sir."

"Oh," Ishie's voice sounded shy. "And no speech prepared. But . . . well, Mike and I have been pulling the cloth—I mean the wool—when we told you about a magneto-ionic effect cancellor. We only did it so that listening ears from Earth would not become wolves after our little lamb. But—you must ask Dr. Millie, she will tell you—what we have been building is a space drive, and I think it will be possible to be somewhere else when the shuttle arrives with its Securities."

He paused. Then: "The people on Earth believe that we are mad scientist space-jackers who kill Thules and make Earth hostage, and I think even though Bessie and her Cow have thrown a monkey in to wrench things a bit, that it will take a few years down there before things come clear, and that we should be lynxed if we had the temerity to return.

"I think," he said softly, "that we must become, in fact, the first space peoples." Then his voice took on a happy lift, "Confusion say when lynx mob runs, is best to high trail."

It had been thirty-two hours since its personnel had retaken the Space Lab, and the Confusor drive units were nearly in place. Fourteen feet long by eighteen inches in diameter, they looked very much like a group of stove pipes arranged in a circular pattern around the engineering quarters, braced from wall to wall.

The drive would give them only a tenth of a gee—but their velocity would compound per second per second, and within minutes of the time that the drive was turned on they could be long kilometers from the spot where the Security shuttle was scheduled to arrive.

It would not be a jack-rabbit leap that took them from orbit, but their tenth of a gee would compound continuously for as long as they cared to keep it thrusting. It opened to them the entire vast storage house of the solar system—possibly even the stars. Stopping to explore would mean turning about at the half-way point to use the same thrust as a slow-down brake.

Their shielding would be sufficient for permanent protection on the way, for the necessity for shielding decreased on the square law as they left Sol, and the former three month safety factor would not apply. If heavier shielding became necessary, it would be devised as needed.

HOT ROD and the pile had been fastened with extra acceleration cables, and later, drive units would be attached to them for added maneuverability.

There were those on board who thought of the solar system as hostile; but to most it was a challenge, amenable to solution. "Man has always adapted environments to himself," Perk had opined dryly during the conference. "Surely our technology will make us more able, rather than less, in this respect."

And there were those on board who felt they should go only a short distance and then return secretly to Earth by ones and twos to help solve the problems there.

That, Mike thought, as he and Ishie, Paul, Tombu and Millie worked on completing the installation of the drive units, was something the peoples of Earth should be allowed to handle for themselves. *You can't give a man freedom,* he thought. *It's something he wins and cherishes—or doesn't have.*

Abruptly he turned to Ishie. "You don't happen to be a psychiatrist, do you Ishie? Or a brain surgeon?" he asked. "We can't just dump those Security cats overboard, but I sure hate to drag 'em along like they are."

"Sorry, Mike." Ishie leaned back against a drive unit. "Techniques of brainwashing are a bit out of my line. Besides, Confusion say those who run from wolf pack have better chance if they leave some meat behind for the wolves to fight over. We *are* going to dump them overboard. I've already spoken to Captain Nails about it. We shan't leave until about twenty minutes before the Security shuttle arrives. Then we'll drop them out the airlock. In suits, of course," he added, "with come-on signals. Then we'll take off and see whether Security takes care of its own."

There was a possibility, Mike felt grimly, that perhaps Security wouldn't take care of its own. But then he asked himself, did he really care? And found it very difficult to come up with an answer. But he realized with vast respect that the master of Confusion was not himself confused as to the issues before them.

"It's lucky for us," he said, "that you happened to pick this time to be aboard, Ishie. Your work might have gone more smoothly if you had waited for the next go-around."

Ishie grinned, for once slightly embarrassed. "It wasn't luck, Mike. It took a lot of pulling of the wires. I expected that with HOT ROD coming into operation, some sort of play would be attempted. I've met Security before."

Across the circular floor, Millie began to hum a soft tune as she wielded a soldering iron. Tombu joined her more lustily while he wrestled with a recalcitrant bolt.

Mike joined in from where he squatted beside Ishie, and suddenly Paul burst into the song, his deep baritone leading the wailing *Spaceman's Lament* in an extra folk beat:

> *The captain spoke of stars and bars*
> *Of far-off places like maybe Mars*
> *But the slipsticks slip on this ship of ours—*
> *And we'll get where I wasn't going . . ."*

Ishie looked at each of them fondly; then he pictured the bridge where Nails Andersen commanded. He might not be as quick on his feet in a fight as the others, but sturdy as an oak and as dependable; and Bessie—who had seen what was coming and planned a counterattack even before it started—and had had sense enough not just to blank the Cow, but to have it spill out garbage as a distraction. He thought of pudgy Claude LaValle defending his animals and his ship with a hypodermic; of Perk and Jerry . . . of an entire shipload of people who had devoted their lives to developing their brains and their know-how, and who were in the habit of using both.

It was a good ship's complement, he thought. Confusion would be happy at the Space People that chance had put aboard the ship.

Then he corrected himself. Chance? Every person aboard had earned his right to be there by the demands he had made on himself since childhood.

Confusion say, he told himself wryly, that these are the real Confusors of Confusion.

Then he joined his small, off-key voice in the chorus of the song:

> *There's a sky-trail leading from here to there*
> *And another yonder showing*
> *But when we get to the end of the run*
> *It will be where I wasn't going. . . .*

EPILOGUE

Mike hunched over the console of the Calf, the components of the intricate part he was designing appearing and being erased at his command on the screen before him.

"Ask the Cow . . ." he began, then with a flip of his hand erased the entire circuit. "It won't do," he thought.

He rose and stretched, then, scuffling his bare toes in the real grass carpeting, he strolled to the edge of the small lake that centered his dome. For a minute he stood staring down at the ebb and flow of the lake's myriad marine life, luxuriating in the one gee field that made the open lake possible, and that was a recent development of The Confusor drive principle.

The maze of components that handled the gravity and other automaticities necessary to the closed ecology of the dome were buried in a ten foot thick floor beneath his feet, along with an emergency air supply, cryogenically stored. On the other side of the floor, upside down to the area where he strolled, an equal area was growing into a tiny forest where small animals abounded.

Taking his time, Mike wandered through the lush plantings that even on this side divided one area from another. They were lighted by hidden solar spectral lamps that gave the dome measured quantities of each of the spectral lines from the sun, providing the necessary health-giving rays that at this distance could not be derived with sufficient intensity from the sunlight itself.

As he reached the laminated glass wall of the dome, glints of light outside caught his eye, and he stopped to watch a game of spaceball. Eight and ten years olds, he decided, from the way they were maneuvering—adept at the motions of three dimensional and weightless action, but a little slow on the uptake from the other side's strategems. At that, they're better than I am, he admitted to himself; but then, they'd been raised going from one gee to zero gee and back again, and their ease of motion was based on learned reactions. Too, today's form-fitting, scuba-style suits with their light drive-packs and air-recycling systems—even though they still had fish-bowl helmets—were a far cry from the bulky space armor in which he'd learned to maneuver in space.

This laminated glass dome itself was a far cry from the original homes they'd lasered out of the centers of asteroids; or from the later bubbles they'd learned to make by plating out steel from the asteroids onto bubble forms —developing the cathode-sputtering techniques that were now the basic structural methods of the Belt. It wasn't until granite asteroids had been located—about ten years back—that it had become possible to use the cathode-sputtering techniques to create the laminated glass domes that now made Belt living really magnificent, bringing the stars and Sol into your home as wall decorations.

Far off to his right a huge ball glinted in the distant sunlight, drifting slowly past—another Venusberg on its way to Ganymede where the five mile chunk of frozen carbon dioxide would be evaporated to provide oxygen for breathing, carbon for food, and the many valuable organic chemical products that were part of its make up.

Millie appeared quietly at his side as he watched the everchanging panorama without.

"It's almost time to leave," she said softly. "We promised to join the others to beam a message to Earth on their 25th Freedom Day anniversary. It's 500 kilometers, and we're due in twenty minutes."

He nodded slowly. Twenty-five years. It had taken Earth a time to work herself out of the vast confusion, and it had been touch and go for a while. Probably more go than had been apparent on the surface, he decided, for once the Cow and her cohorts had done their work, mankind had taken a good look at Security, and a stubbornness had set in.

Had that been the major factor? Or had it been the Confusor drive? He didn't know. The Cow had beamed specs for the Confusor into every memory bank on the planet before they left. Still, it had been nearly five years before the groundlings had developed the automobile-sized ship with the air recycling system that made possible a trip from anywhere to anywhere for individuals.

After that, the flight from the planet had grown on an exponential curve, as every man jack and his family—at least the new generation—had started out on a trip of exploration of his own.

The Belt was getting crowded now, Mike felt. Automated factories were everywhere; trading centers were within the reach of anyone. A man didn't feel on his own out here any more. . . .

Oh, well. The starship was nearly complete—more a string of bubble domes anchor-tubed to a hundred-mile-diameter Space Lab-drive-center-gathering-area than a ship—but ready for the stars.

Would they find other intelligent life forms out there, he wondered? And if they did—would they be able to communicate with that other life?

He grinned wryly. Hell, he thought, we've just about learned to communicate with a computer—and that's an electromagnetic-mechanical monster, and an alien life form if there ever was one, even if we did build it in the first place. Anybody—but, anybody—who could learn

to handle the stubborn, literal-minded, syllogistically or-
iented, faster-than-man reactive Cow ought to be able to
learn.

Then he corrected himself. We didn't learn to handle
the Cow, he thought. We taught the Cow how to be
handled by us—and that's different.

"What are you grinning so Cheshire cat-like at?" Mil-
lie asked.

He slipped his arm around her slender waist, and they
stood a minute looking out into the infinite reaches of
space.

"I was thinking," he said. "We've had a lot of fun out
here. We've raised a lot of families; developed a lot of
know-how; watched Earth free herself and come out to
join us.

"It may not be where we were going, but I'm glad we
got here.

"But, Millie—where is it we aren't going now?"

FRITZ LEIBER

Just $1.25 each

The Big Time
Green Millennium
Swords Against Death
Swords and Deviltry
Swords Against Wizardry
Swords in the Mist
The Swords of Lankhmar
You're All Alone

Available wherever paperbacks are sold or use this coupon.

Ursula K. LeGuin

City of Illusion $1.50

Left Hand of Darkness $1.75

Planet of Exile $1.50

Rocannon's World $1.50

Available wherever paperbacks are sold or use this coupon:

33 H

A.E. VAN VOGT

Just $1.25 each

Children of Tomorrow

The Worlds of A.E. van Vogt

Quest for the Future

The Silkie

The Universe Maker

The Weapon Shops of Isher

11
NOVELS BY
ROBERT A. HEINLEIN

$1.25 each

Between Planets

Citizen of the Galaxy

Have Space Suit-Will Travel

Red Planet

Rocket Ship Galileo

The Rolling Stones

Space Cadet

The Star Beast

Time for the Stars

Tunnel in the Sky

The Worlds of Robert A. Heinlein

Available wherever paperbacks are sold or use this coupon.

SCIENCE FICTION from the GREAT YEARS

Just $1.25 each

Alien Planet Pratt

A Brand New World Cummings

Galaxy Primes Smith

Little Fuzzy Piper

Metropolis Von Harbou

Mightiest Machine Campbell

The Moon is Hell Campbell

SF: The Great Years, Part I Pohl

SF: The Great Years, Part II Pohl

Ultimate Weapon Campbell

Available wherever paperbacks are sold or use this coupon.

ACE SCIENCE FICTION SPECIALS

Just $1.25 each

#1—From the Legend of Biel Staton
#2—Red Tide Tarzan & Chapman
#3—Endless Voyage Bradley
#4—The Invincible Lem
#5—Growing Up In Tier 3000 Gotschalk
#6—Challenge the Hellmaker Richmond
#7—Tournament of Thorns Swann
#8—Fifth Head of Cerberse Wolfe

Available wherever paperbacks are sold or use this coupon.

64A